14 ¾. We Now Return to Our Regularly Scheduled
Chapter (Already in Progress . . .)   80

15. Bad Hair Night   82

16. Who's Afraid of the Big Bad Beehive?   89

17. All Tied Up   93

18. Robo-George and the Harold 2000   99

19. Tra-La-Luuunatics   105

20. You Axed for It   111

21. The Woothless Wevenge of
the Wicked Wedgie Woman   114

22. They Can't   120

23. The Origin of Captain Underpants   125

24. The Placenta Effect   133

25. The Incredibly Graphic Violence
Chapter (in Flip-O-Rama™)   137

26. Reverse Psychology 2   157

27. Reverse Reverse Psychology   164

28. To Make a Long Story Short   168

29. Better Living Through Hypnosis   169

CAPTAIN UNDERPANTS

TwoTURBO-CHARGED Novels in One

FULL COLOUR!

SCHOLASTIC

"Imagination is more
important than knowledge."
–Albert Einstein

Published in the UK by Scholastic Children's Books, 2021
Euston House, 24 Eversholt Street, London, NWI IDB
A division of Scholastic Limited

London – New York – Toronto – Sydney – Auckland
Mexico City – New Delhi – Hong Kong

Captain Underpants and the Wrath of the Wicked Wedgie Woman
First published in the US by Scholastic Inc., 2001
Copyright © Dav Pilkey, 2001

Captain Underpants and the Big, Bad Battle of the Bionic
Booger Boy, Part I: The Night of the Nasty Nostril Nuggets
First published in the US by Scholastic Inc., 2003
Copyright © Dav Pilkey, 2003

ISBN 978 0702 30677 8

A CIP catalogue record for this book is available from the British Library.

Printed and bound in China
Papers used by Scholastic Children's Books are made
from wood grown in sustainable forests.

1 3 5 7 9 10 8 6 4 2

www.scholastic.co.uk

FULL COLOUR

CAPTAIN UNDERPANTS

AND THE WRATH OF THE Wicked WEDGie WOMAN

The Fifth Epic Novel by

DAV PILKEY

with color by Jose Garibaldi

SCHOLASTIC

CHAPTERS

FOREWORD:
The Trouble with Captain Underpants   7

1. George and Harold   11
2. Ms. Ribble's Big News   15
3. When You Care Enough to Send the Very Best 17
4. Captain Underpants and the Wrath
   of the Wicked Wedgie Woman   21
5. The Wrath of Ms. Ribble   31
6. The Retirement Card   35
7. Reverse Psychology   39
8. The Party   43
9. Freaky Weeky   49
10. The Big Wedding   54
11. The Refreshments   61
12. Ribble's Revenge   71
13. A Bad Idea   73
14. The Return of the 3-D Hypno-Ring   75
14 1/2. We Interrupt This Chapter to Bring
       You This Important Message   78

The TRUBBLE WiTH
CAPTAIN UnderPants

NOW it can BE TOLD ! ! ! ! ! !

--A inFORMashonal comic By George and Harold.

ONse upon a time There were Two cool Kids named George and Harold.

We Kick Butt.

Me Too.

BuT They had a mean principle named MR. Krupp.

Come over Here, Bubs!

No way

One time George and Harold Hipnotized MR. KRUPP with the 3-D HipNO-RiNG™

You wiLL oBey our comand.

O.K.

zAP.

George and Harold made him think he was A GReAT super Hero Named Captain Underpants.

LooK--- I'm CAPTAIN UnderPants!

HA HA HA

It was funny at first, But then mr. KRUPP Jumped out the Window.

Hey where do you Think Your going?

To fight crime, ok?

George and Harold Had to chase After Him so he wouldén't get killed and hurt.

Come over Here, Bub!

No WAY!

They had many advenchures with Lots of inapropreate HUMOR.

DiApers and Toilets and poop... OH my!

PP

Then one day MR. Krupp Askidentelly drank super Juice.

super power Juice

GLUB GLUB

Now He gots super powers. He can Fly Too!

TRA-LA Laaaaa!!!

Two things you half to be careful about is: water and finger snaps.

H2O

SNAP

For if you snap your fingers by MR. Krupp...

SNAP

...He turns into Captain Underpants.

TRA-LA LAAAA!

And if you pore water on Captain Underpantses head...

H2O

...He turns back into MR. Krupp.

BLAH BLAH BLAH

So... If you see MR. Krupp, don't snap your fingers or you'll be sorry.

SNAP

And if you see Captain Underpants, don't pore no water on his head or youll be SORRYER!!!

H2O

Remember- This is **TOP-SECRET** so don't tell Anybody!!!

Treehouse comix

INC.

CHAPTER 1
GEORGE AND HAROLD

This is George Beard and Harold Hutchins. George is the kid on the left with the tie and the flat-top. Harold is the one on the right with the T-shirt and the bad haircut. Remember that now.

PEOPLE – PLEASE WEAR YOUR SOCKS ON THE GYM FLOOR

At most schools, the teachers try to emphasize "the three **R**s" (**R**eading, '**R**iting, and '**R**ithmetic). But George and Harold's teacher, Ms. Ribble, was more concerned with enforcing what she called "the three **S**s" (**S**it down, **S**hut your pie holes, and **S**TOP DRIVING ME CRAZY!).

While this was unfortunate for all of her students, it was especially bad for

George and Harold, because they were very
imaginative boys.

You see, imagination was not really
encouraged at George and Harold's school—
in fact, it was discouraged. Imagination
would only get you a one-way ticket to the
principal's office.

This was sad for George and Harold,
because they didn't get straight As, they
weren't sports stars, and they could barely
walk down the hallway without getting
into trouble . . .

See what I mean?!!?

But George and Harold had one thing
that most of the other folks at Jerome
Horwitz Elementary School didn't have:
imagination. They were *full* of it! And one
day they would use that imagination to
save the entire human race from being
overthrown by a crazed woman with even
crazier super powers.

But before I can tell you that story, I have
to tell you *this* story . . .

CHAPTER 2
MS. RIBBLE'S BIG NEWS

One fine day, George and Harold's homeroom teacher, Ms. Ribble, entered the classroom looking a bit meaner than usual.

"Alright, settle down!" shouted Ms. Ribble. "I have some bad news: I'm retiring."

"Hooray!" cried the children.

"Not today!" snapped Ms. Ribble. "At the end of the school year!"

"Aww, *maaaan*," moaned the children.

"But the staff is throwing a retirement party for me today . . ." said Ms. Ribble.

"Hooray!" cried the children.

". . . during recess," said Ms. Ribble.

"Aww, *maaaan*," moaned the children.

"There will be lots of free ice cream!"
said Ms. Ribble.

"Hooray!" cried the children.

"My favorite flavor: *chunky tofu*!" said
Ms. Ribble.

"Aww, *maaaan*," moaned the children.

"But first," said Ms. Ribble, "it's time for
something fun!"

"Hooray!" cried the children.

"You all get to make 'Happy Retirement'
cards for me!" said Ms. Ribble.

"Aww, *maaaan*," moaned the children.

CHAPTER 3
WHEN YOU CARE
ENOUGH TO SEND
THE VERY BEST

Ms. Ribble went around the classroom handing out envelopes, sheets of construction paper, and butterfly stencils to all of the children. Then she wrote a poem on the chalkboard.

"Alright, take out your crayons," said Ms. Ribble harshly. "I want you to use stencils to make a yellow butterfly on the front of your cards. When you're done, copy this poem on the inside."

"Can we make up our own poems?" asked Melvin Sneedly.

"No!" snapped Ms. Ribble.

"Do we have to use stencils?" asked Aaron Mancini.

"YES!" yelled Ms. Ribble.

"Can we make our butterflies purple?" asked Stephanie Yarkoff.

"NO!" screamed Ms. Ribble. "Butterflies are yellow! Everyone knows that!"

While the rest of the class worked on their cards, George and Harold had a better idea.

"Let's make Ms. Ribble a comic book instead!" said George.

"Yeah!" said Harold. "We can make it all about her. It'll be cool!"

So that's just what they did.

CHAPTER 4
CAPTAIN UNDERPANTS AND THE WRATH OF THE WICKED WEDGIE WOMAN

By George Beard
And Harold Hutchins

CAPTAIN UNDERPANTS

And the WRATH OF the Wicked Wedgie Woman

Story By George Beard • Pictures By Harold Hutchins

Onse upon a time there was A really mean teacher named ms. Ribble who was very mean.

GRRRRR

I'm Am evil!

She gave us lots of homework and yelled at us all the time.

Read 250 Pages for A test!

AW MAN!

One Time at chrismas vacashion she gave everybody 41 Book Reports.

Ho Ho Ho!

Dec. 25

Wake up... It's time to open up your presints!

I cant! I half to do my homework!!!

After chrismas every-body turned in A Big Pile of book Reports.

HAW-HAW HAW!

Then something terible Happened.

CRASH

Help!

MS. RiBBLe WAS BARied in A mounten of Book Reports

Shes REALLY most SinSERLY Dead.

No Shes Not. We can Re-Build Her...

DocteR

We can mAke Her better than she wAs. ...Faster... stronger... eviler!!!

Bionic LEG

Bionic LEG

operating table

surgen

Bionic Hair

Bionic ARM

Bionic ARM

When MS. RiBBLe got out of The hospiteL, She hAd Bionic Powers.

I will take over the world. HAW HAW HAW!!!

So she mAde a eviL Costume.

SNip SNip

Her Bionic Beehive Hairdoo opened up to Reveal a eviL wedgie ROBO-CLAW.

oucHies!

HAW HAW NoBody cAn stop me now!

inosent Bystander

HeLp! wedgie Woman is in the teachers Lounge. she just drAnk all The coffee and now shes giving the gym teacher A KiLLer-weDgie!!!

OH, The HoRRoR!! She better make A Fresh pot!!!

principeL

And abel to Leap tall bildings without getting A wedgie.

TRA-LA LAAAAA!

RATS

So Wedgie Woman went to the store to buy some spray starch.

NEW SPRAY STARCH

STARCH is The Enemy of underwear!

WARNING: DO NOT spray this product on your underwear OR youll Be sorry!

wedgie woman sprayed.

Gotcha!

HEY!

SSSSS

OH NO! My underpants is ALL stiff and uncomfertable!

HAW HAW

captain underpants tried to push the buttons on his utility waistband But they were broke!! HE WAS POWERLESS!

I'm DOOMED!

SPLASH

Swiming Pool

The kids PORed FABRIC softener in the pool.

FABRIC softener

Swim

sudenly the starch got washed away. HOORAY!!!

my underpants is soft and cottony onse Again!!!

HALLY-LOOYA!!

Swiming

thanks Kids

No problemo.

Soon captain Underpants Found wedgie woman.

Remember me?

Get Him ROBO-CLAW

NOTISE: Any simalarities
to actual persons (living
or dead) is very, very
unforchenate.

CHAPTER 5
THE WRATH OF
MS. RIBBLE

When Ms. Ribble read the comic book that George and Harold had made, she was furious.

"Boys!" she yelled. "You've just earned yourselves a one-way ticket to the principal's office!"

"But all we did was use our imaginations!" said George.

"You're not allowed to do that in this school!" snapped Ms. Ribble. "Didn't you read chapter 1?"

George and Harold gathered their things, and soon they were sitting in the office outside Mr. Krupp's door.

"Mr. Krupp is on the phone," said the school secretary, Miss Anthrope. "Why don't you boys make yourselves useful and copy the 'Friday Memo' for me! You can pass them out to all the classrooms for me while I go to lunch."

"Aww, *maaaan!*" said George.

"*Quit your whining, buster!*" shouted Miss Anthrope. "I want this done by the time I get back, or you'll *both* be sorry!" Miss Anthrope grabbed her coat and stomped out the door.

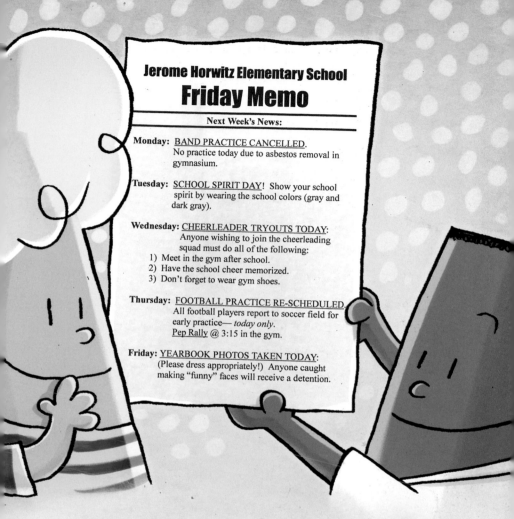

Jerome Horwitz Elementary School
Friday Memo

Next Week's News:

Monday: BAND PRACTICE CANCELLED. No practice today due to asbestos removal in gymnasium.

Tuesday: SCHOOL SPIRIT DAY! Show your school spirit by wearing the school colors (gray and dark gray).

Wednesday: CHEERLEADER TRYOUTS TODAY: Anyone wishing to join the cheerleading squad must do all of the following:
1) Meet in the gym after school.
2) Have the school cheer memorized.
3) Don't forget to wear gym shoes.

Thursday: FOOTBALL PRACTICE RE-SCHEDULED. All football players report to soccer field for early practice— *today only*. Pep Rally @ 3:15 in the gym.

Friday: YEARBOOK PHOTOS TAKEN TODAY: (Please dress appropriately!) Anyone caught making "funny" faces will receive a detention.

George and Harold looked at the "Friday Memo." It was a weekly newsletter that told all about the events of the upcoming week.

"Hey," said George. "Miss Anthrope's computer is still on. Y'wanna make a few changes to this newsletter?"

"Why not?" said Harold.

Friday Memo

Next Week's News:

Monday: SCHOOL CANCELLED.
No classes today due to lack of interest.

Tuesday: NATIONAL WEAR YOUR PAJAMAS TO
SCHOOL AND PICK YOUR NOSE DAY!
Show you care by wearing your pajamas to
school (and picking your nose).

Wednesday: CHEERLEADER TRYOUTS TODAY:
Anyone wishing to join the cheerleading
squad must do all of the following:
1) Eat ten whole cloves of raw garlic
2) Draw a mustache on your face with permanent markers.
3) Tape a three-day-old egg-salad sandwich to your head.

Thursday: FOOTBALL PRACTICE RE-SCHEDULED.
All football players report to teachers' lounge
for early practice.
Food Fight @ 12:15 in the lunchroom.

Friday: YEARBOOK PHOTOS TAKEN TODAY:
(Please wear Bumblebee costumes).
Also, whoever makes the funniest face wins
a free pizza party for their class.

So George and Harold typed up their own version of the Jerome Horwitz Elementary School "Friday Memo." Then they ran off copies for all the students in the school.

CHAPTER 6
THE RETIREMENT CARD

George and Harold were gathering their new-and-improved "Friday Memo" copies into small piles when Principal Krupp came into the office.

"Hey!" Mr. Krupp shouted. "What are you two troublemakers doing in here?"

"Miss Anthrope told us to pass the 'Friday Memo' out to all the classrooms," said George innocently.

"Well, make it snappy!" yelled Principal Krupp.

Suddenly, Harold got a sneaky idea. He took out the blank piece of construction paper that Ms. Ribble had given him earlier.

"Hey, Mr. Krupp," said Harold, "will you sign this retirement card for our teacher?"

Mr. Krupp grabbed the card from Harold and eyed it suspiciously.

"This card is *blank*!" Mr. Krupp growled.

"I know," said Harold. "Our class is going to decorate it later. We wanted you to be the first to sign it."

"Well, alright then," said Mr. Krupp.
He opened the card and quickly scribbled

Signed, Mr. Krupp

on the inside. Then he stormed out of
the office.

"What are you gonna do with that?"
asked George.

"You'll see," said Harold, smiling.

CHAPTER 7
REVERSE PSYCHOLOGY

George and Harold passed out the "Friday
Memo" and made it back to their classroom
just in time for Ms. Ribble's retirement party.
George quickly changed the letters around
on the sign outside the door, while Harold
wrote a special greeting on Mr. Krupp's card
and stuffed it into the envelope.

"*HEY, BUBS!*" shouted Mr. Krupp as he stormed down the hall. "What do you kids think you're doing?"

"We're going to Ms. Ribble's retirement party," said George.

"That's what *YOU* think, smart guy!" said Mr. Krupp. "Ms. Ribble showed me that comic book you boys made about her. And now I catch you changing the letters around on another sign! You boys aren't going to any party . . . you're going STRAIGHT to the detention room!"

"Well *fine*," said Harold. "Then we're not gonna give Ms. Ribble the card our class made for her!"

Mr. Krupp quickly swiped the card out of Harold's hand.

"A-HA!" he shouted. "I'm going to make SURE she gets this card! I'm going to give it to her *MYSELF*!"

"Aww, *maaaan*!" said Harold.

SWIPE

George and Harold walked down the hallway toward the detention room.

"Wow," said George. "That was pretty cool how you got Mr. Krupp to deliver that phony card for you."

"Yep," said Harold. "I used *reverse psychology* on him!"

"I've gotta try that sometime," said George. "By the way, what did you write on that card?"

"You'll see," said Harold, smiling.

CHAPTER 8
THE PARTY

Ms. Ribble's retirement party started off bad, and just got worse. First, Ms. Ribble forced the class to sing a corny song to her. By the time she was done yelling at the boys for singing off-key, the chunky tofu ice cream was melted.

Everybody had to eat it anyway.

Then the children handed in their "Happy Retirement" cards. Ms. Ribble ripped several of the cards up because some of the children had mistakenly drawn polka-dots on their butterflies. One unfortunate boy had also drawn a happy smiling sunshine on his card, and he had to stand in the corner.

Finally, Mr. Krupp stepped forward and handed Ms. Ribble the card he had snatched from Harold's hand.

"I went to a lot of trouble to get this for you," Mr. Krupp said gallantly.

Ms. Ribble tore the envelope open and read the card out loud:

"You're One *Hot Mama*!" said Ms. Ribble, with a shocked look on her face.

"Eeeeeeeeew!" cried the children.

She opened the card and read the inside.
"Will you marry me? Signed, Mr. Krupp."
"Eeeeeeeeeeeeeeeeeeeeeeeeeeeewww!"
cried the children. The teachers gasped.
Then the room grew silent. Ms. Ribble glared
over at Mr. Krupp, who had turned bright
red and began sweating profusely.

He tried to speak. He tried to tell her
it was all a big mistake. He tried to say
SOMETHING . . . but all that came out was
"B-B-Bubba bobba hob-hobba-hobba wah-wah."

46

"Er, ummm, *congratulations*," said Mr. Meaner, as he patted Mr. Krupp's sweaty, shivering shoulder.

"Yes! CONGRATULATIONS!" shouted Miss Anthrope. "This will be the best wedding in the whole world! We can have it here at the school . . . a week from Saturday! I'll plan everything! You lovebirds don't have to worry about a thing!"

"Er-uh . . . great . . . thanks," said Ms.
Ribble, still looking quite angry and confused.
"B-B-Bubba bobba hob-hobba-hobba
wah-wah," said Mr. Krupp.

48

CHAPTER 9
FREAKY WEEKY

The following week at Jerome Horwitz Elementary School was definitely one of the weirdest ones they'd had in a while. For example: None of the kids showed up for school on Monday. But Mr. Krupp didn't even seem to notice.

"Hey, where is everybody today?" asked Mr. Rected.

"B-B-Bubba bobba hob-hobba-hobba wah-wah," said Mr. Krupp.

On Tuesday everybody did show up . . .
in their pajamas!

"Why is everybody picking their noses?"
asked Miss Fitt.

"B-B-Bubba bobba hob-hobba-hobba
wah-wah," said Mr. Krupp.

On Wednesday, for some strange reason, the whole school smelled like garlic and rotten egg-salad sandwiches (especially some of the girls).

"Boy," said Ms. Guided, "the styles today sure are getting bizarre."

"B-B-Bubba bobba hob-hobba-hobba wah-wah," said Mr. Krupp.

Thursday was, without a doubt, a complete and total disaster.

"There's a food fight in the lunchroom!" shouted Mr. Rustworthy. "And the football team is destroying the teachers' lounge!"

"B-B-Bubba bobba hob-hobba-hobba wah-wah," said Mr. Krupp.

Now, *nobody* was sure what happened on Friday. Apparently, there was a mix-up with the dress code and the yearbook photos.

"Our school pictures are ruined!" shouted Ms. Dayken.

"B-B-Bubba bobba hob-hobba-hobba wah-wah," said Mr. Krupp.

Yes, it was a freaky week, alright. But the big wedding was only a day away . . . and things were about to get REALLY freaky!

CHAPTER 10
THE BIG WEDDING

It was Saturday, the day of the big wedding. Miss Anthrope, true to her word, had taken care of everything. In just one week, she had transformed the gymnasium into a beautiful wedding hall, complete with food, decorations, and even a six-foot-tall ice sculpture.

All of the children were dressed in their finest clothes. (Harold even wore a tie!)

"Man," said George, "I can't believe we have to go to school on *SATURDAY*!"

"I know," said Harold. "Why couldn't they have had this wedding during Monday's math test?"

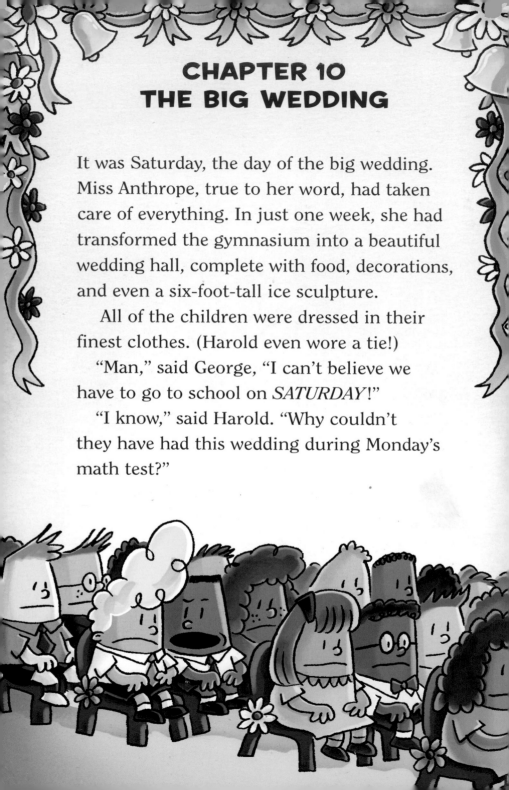

Soon the organist began to play. The rabbi walked down the aisle. He approached George and Harold and stopped to talk to the boys.

"I've heard a lot about you two," said the rabbi, "and I don't want you boys playing any of your tricks today."

"Silly Rabbi," said George, "tricks are for kids!"

Believe it or not, George and Harold had not planned any pranks for the big wedding. They had no Joy Buzzers up their sleeves . . . no squirting flowers in their lapels . . . and no whoopee cushions on their chairs. They were on their best behavior. Nothing could go wrong today!

In no time at all, Ms. Ribble and Mr. Krupp were standing in front of the rabbi, looking quite ill. The rabbi asked Mr. Krupp if he would take Ms. Ribble to be his lawfully wedded wife.

"B-B-Bubba bobba hob-hobba-hobba wah-wah," said Mr. Krupp.

Then the rabbi asked Ms. Ribble if she would take Mr. Krupp to be her husband.

There was a long silence. Everyone leaned forward. Ms. Ribble looked nervously from side to side.

Suddenly, she shouted out at the top of her lungs, *"NOOOOOOOOOOOOOOOO!"*

Ms. Ribble turned to Mr. Krupp and jabbed her finger into his shoulder. "Listen, Krupp," she said. "I *can't* marry you."

"Hooray! —er, I mean —*aww, that's too bad*!" said Mr. Krupp.

"You're a mean, cruel, and vicious man," said Ms. Ribble, "and I respect that. It's just . . . it's just . . ."

"Just what?" asked Mr. Krupp.

"It's just your *nose*!" said Ms. Ribble. "You've got the most *ridiculous* nose — I've never seen anything quite like it! I just couldn't marry somebody with such a silly nose."

Mr. Krupp got angry. "Well *fine*!" he
shouted. "I didn't want to marry you anyway!
It was all George and Harold's fault. They
tricked us!"

Suddenly, everybody in the gymnasium
turned and looked at George and Harold.

"Time to go," said George.

CHAPTER 11
THE REFRESHMENTS

As George and Harold turned to leave the gymnasium, they heard the loud thumps of cleated wedding boots clomping down the aisle toward them.

"I'M GONNA GRIND THOSE KIDS INTO HEADCHEESE!" screamed Ms. Ribble as she lunged for the two boys.

George and Harold screamed and ran to
the back of the room near the refreshments.
There they hid behind two large wooden
pillars.

Ms. Ribble approached the pillars and
grasped them with her mighty hands. With
a horrible roar, she pushed the right pillar
over. It landed on the back of the luncheon
table, causing the front of the table to flip
high into the air. Unfortunately, this sent
all of the food flying into the crowd.

The creamy candied carrots clobbered the kindergartners. The fatty fried fish fritters flipped onto the first graders. The sweet-n-sour spaghetti squash splattered the second graders.

Three thousand thawing thimbleberries thudded the third graders. Five hundred frosted fudgy fruitcakes flogged the fourth graders. And fifty-five fistfuls of fancy french-fried frankfurters flattened the fifth graders.

By now you're probably worried that the wedding guests had nothing to drink with their lovely appetizers. Well, rest assured, the second pillar took care of that. Ms. Ribble pushed the left pillar into the fresh fruit display, causing it to topple over, sending

two large watermelons crashing down into two oversized punch bowls. This created two enormous splashes of tropical fruit-flavored punch, which rained down upon the wedding guests like a torrential downpour.

Now, no wedding is complete without a wedding cake. And when Ms. Ribble kicked the ice sculpture over, the resulting crash sent the beautiful double-deckered cake flipping high into the air, right over Ms. Ribble's head.

"I'VE GOT YOU NOW!" screamed Ms. Ribble, as she grabbed George and Harold by their neckties.

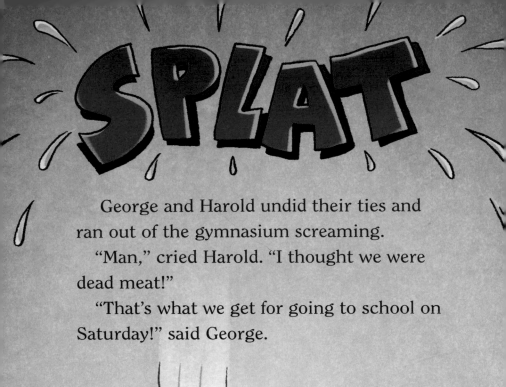

SPLAT

George and Harold undid their ties and ran out of the gymnasium screaming.

"Man," cried Harold. "I thought we were dead meat!"

"That's what we get for going to school on Saturday!" said George.

CHAPTER 12
RIBBLE'S REVENGE

As you might imagine, George and Harold were nervous about going back to class on Monday. But for some strange reason, Ms. Ribble seemed happy to see them.

"Good morning, boys," Ms. Ribble chirped with a giant, evil, toothy grin. "Come here . . . I've got something to show you!"

"Uh-oh," said George. "She's smiling — that *can't* be a good sign!"

George and Harold cautiously approached Ms. Ribble's desk.

"I took the liberty of adjusting your grades last weekend," said Ms. Ribble. "You'll be happy to know that all your grades have just dropped from Bs and Cs to *Fs* and *Gs*."

"Oh, *NO!*" George gasped. "Not *Fs* and *Gs!* Hey, what's a *G*?"

"It's the only grade *lower* than an *F*!" said Ms. Ribble.

"There's no such grade as a *G*," said Harold.

"There is now, bub!" said Ms. Ribble. "Looks like you're both going to *FLUNK* the FOURTH GRADE!!! Won't that be fun?"

"No way," said George. *"That's not fair!"*

"Life ain't fair," said Ms. Ribble. "Get used to it!"

CHAPTER 13
A BAD IDEA

That afternoon, George and Harold sat in their tree house feeling sorry for themselves.

"She can't get away with that," said George. "We've got to tell somebody about this."

"Nobody's going to believe us," said Harold.

"Well, there is *one* thing we can do," said George. He opened the drawer to their drawing table and searched through the pennies, paper clips, dried spitballs, and rubber bands. Then he pulled out a dusty plastic ring with some gum stuck on it. It was the 3-D Hypno-Ring.

"Oh, no!" said Harold. "I thought we threw that thing away!"

"We just threw the instructions away," said George. "But I remember how it works."

"Do you *remember* what happened the LAST TIME WE USED IT?" asked Harold.

"Yeah," said George. "But we were fooling around last time. This time we'll be serious. We won't make any mistakes! All we have to do is hypnotize her into changing our grades back to normal. That's all!"

"I don't know . . ." said Harold. "It sounds like a bad idea to me!"

"Worse than *FLUNKING* the fourth grade?" asked George.

"Good point," said Harold.

CHAPTER 14
THE RETURN OF THE
3-D HYPNO-RING

The next day at school, George and Harold stayed behind while the rest of the class went outside for recess.

"What are you punks still doing here?" asked Ms. Ribble.

"Ummmm," said George nervously. "Er, we wanted to show you this really cool ring."

"Yeah," said Harold. "If you look closely at it, you can see a funny picture."

"Well, hold it still," said Ms. Ribble, as she stared at the ring intently.

"I have to move it back and forth," said George, "or you won't be able to see the picture."

Ms. Ribble's eyes followed the ring back and forth . . . back and forth . . . back and forth . . . back and forth . . .

"You are getting sleepy," said George.

"Veeery sleepy," said Harold.

Ms. Ribble yawned. Her eyes began to droop.

"I'mmssooosleeeeepyyy," she said, as she slowly closed her eyes.

"In a moment," said George, "I will snap my fingers. Then you will be hypnotized."

"Sssssoooosssslllleeeeeeeeepyyyyyyy," mumbled Ms. Ribble.

SNAP!

"Now," said Harold, "you must listen very . . ."

CHAPTER 14 1/2
WE INTERRUPT THIS
CHAPTER TO BRING YOU
THIS IMPORTANT
MESSAGE:

"Hello, this is Chim-Chim Diaperbrains . . . er, I mean, this is Ingrid Ashley reporting for Eyewitness News. We have a late-breaking story about a tragic incident that is now occurring in the Pacific Northwest.

"Police have just closed down the Li'l Wiseguy Novelty Company in Walla Walla, Washington. Apparently, this company has been selling very dangerous Hypno-Rings. We now take you live, via satellite, to our reporter, Booger Stinkersquirt, er, I mean, Larry Zarrow, with the latest developments."

"Thanks, Chim-Chim," said Larry. "Reports have poured in from all across the country concerning children who have used the 3-D Hypno-Ring on their friends and family with disastrous results. But the most shocking revelation is the effect that the rings seem to have on *women*.

"Apparently, whenever the ring is used to hypnotize a woman, a mental blunder occurs, causing the woman to do the OPPOSITE of what she is being hypnotized to do.

"Doctors don't know why the ring causes women to have an OPPOSITE reaction, but they are very concerned. If you or someone you love has purchased a 3-D Hypno-Ring, throw it away at once. And whatever you do, PLEASE DON'T USE IT ON A WOMAN!"

CHAPTER 14³/₄
WE NOW RETURN TO
OUR REGULARLY
SCHEDULED CHAPTER
(ALREADY IN PROGRESS . . .)

". . . and when we snap our fingers," George continued, "you will change our grades back to normal."

"Yeah," said Harold. "And you won't do anything crazy, like turn into *Wedgie Woman*."

"And you won't try to destroy Captain Underpants," said George, "or take over the world, either."

"Right!" said Harold. "You'll just change our grades, and that's it!"

George and Harold looked nervously at each other.

"Well," said George, "I think that covers everything."

"Yep," said Harold. "We shouldn't have any more problems from Ms. Ribble."

So the boys snapped their fingers.

SNAP!

CHAPTER 15
BAD HAIR NIGHT

That night, George and Harold camped out in George's tree house.

"I have to drive your mother to work early tomorrow morning," said George's dad. "So you boys are responsible for getting yourselves to school on time."

"OK, Pop," said George.

"We'll be there bright and early, Mr. Beard," said Harold.

It had been a tough day for George and
Harold, and now it was time to relax. George
rolled out the sleeping bags, while Harold
unpacked a box of chocolate donuts, four
cans of orange cream soda, and a big bowl of
Bar-B-Q potato chips. Believe it or not, there
was even a cool Japanese monster movie
playing on TV.

"You know," said George, "life doesn't get
any better than this!"

"Yep," said Harold. "But do you think the
Hypno-Ring actually worked on Ms. Ribble?
She looked a little weird when she came out
of her trance."

"Aaah, she was probably just sleepy," said
George. "Teachers have very stressful jobs,
you know."

"I wonder why?" said Harold.

After the movie, George and Harold
brushed the crumbs out of their sleeping
bags and got ready for bed.

"Let's sleep in our school clothes tonight,"
said George. "That way we won't have to
wake up early to get dressed."

"Good idea," said Harold.

So George turned out the light, and soon
the two boys were drifting off to sleep. After a
few minutes, Harold sat up quickly and
looked around.

"Hey!" he whispered. "What's that noise?"

"I didn't hear anything," said George.

They listened closely.

"Shhh!" said Harold. "There it is again!"

George heard it this time. He reached over and opened the tree house door a crack. All they could hear was the sound of crickets chirping in the night. George opened the door wider, and the boys peeked down.

"AAAUUGH!" roared an evil-looking woman dressed in tight purple vinyl and a mangy-looking fake-fur boa.

George and Harold screamed in horror!

The snarling woman climbed from the ladder into the tree house. George and Harold recognized her immediately in the moonlight.

"Ms. Ribble," George gasped. "What a lovely, uh, *outfit* you have on."

"Who's Ms. Ribble?" the angry lady growled. "My name is *Wedgie Woman*!!!"

George and Harold looked at each other and swallowed hard.

"I understand that you boys have information about Captain Underpants," said Wedgie Woman.

"What makes you say that?" asked Harold.

"I've read your comic books," said the evil villain. "You boys know his strengths, his weaknesses, and I'll bet you even know his SECRET IDENTITY!"

"No way!" said George. "Captain Underpants isn't real . . . He—he's just a cartoon!"

"We'll see about that," Wedgie Woman scoffed.

Wedgie Woman reached out and grasped George's and Harold's arms.

"What do we do now?" cried Harold.

"We can take 'er," said George. "It's not like she has super powers or anything!"

CHAPTER 16
WHO'S AFRAID OF THE BIG BAD BEEHIVE?

The struggle that followed may someday be
remembered as the single most unlucky
thing that ever happened in the history of
the world.

First, George pulled his arm out of Wedgie
Woman's grasp. Then Harold squirmed away,
too. When Wedgie Woman lunged after
them, George crouched down into a ball
behind Wedgie Woman's feet. All it took was
a simple nudge from Harold to send the
ferocious female toppling over backward . . .

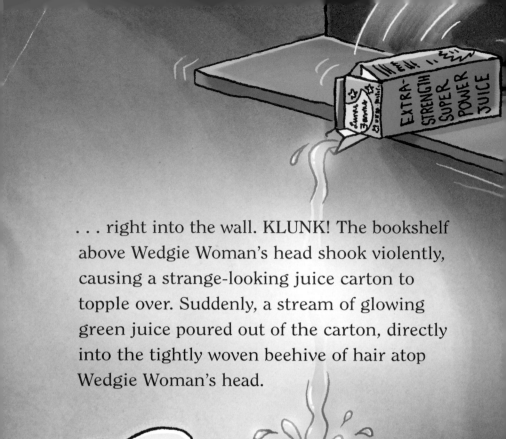

. . . right into the wall. KLUNK! The bookshelf above Wedgie Woman's head shook violently, causing a strange-looking juice carton to topple over. Suddenly, a stream of glowing green juice poured out of the carton, directly into the tightly woven beehive of hair atop Wedgie Woman's head.

"NOOO!" yelled Harold as he grabbed the
juice carton. "This is the juice we got from
that spaceship back in our third book!"

"You mean the one with the annoyingly
long title?" asked George.

"Yeah!" said Harold. "This is Extra-
Strength Super Power Juice! And a whole
bunch of it got in her hair!"

"Don't worry," said George. "None of it got
in her mouth. What's the worst thing that
could happen? Her *hairstyle* would have
super powers?"

"Well," said Harold, "I guess you're right.
That *is* pretty stupid . . . even for one of *our*
stories!"

"It's pretty funny, though," said George.

91

Suddenly, two coiled arms of twisting hair shot out of Wedgie Woman's head and grabbed George and Harold by the back of their underwear, yanking them high into the air.

"You know," said George, "this isn't as funny as I thought it would be."

CHAPTER 17
ALL TIED UP

Wedgie Woman brought George and Harold back to her house and tied the boys tightly to two chairs.

"Tell me the secret identity of Captain Underpants!" screamed Wedgie Woman.

"No way!" said George.

"Hmmmm," said Wedgie Woman. "You want to do this the hard way? *No problem!*"

Wedgie Woman's hair began uncoiling itself. Several twisted locks of hair stretched out into the living room and started taking apart the television, the computer, and a ThighMaster®.

Other tangled coils reached into
the kitchen and began dismantling the
dishwasher, the toaster oven, and a
Ronco Food Dehydrator.

"What are you doing?" asked Harold.

"If you want to make robots," said
Wedgie Woman, "you gotta
break a few small
appliances!"

MEANEST
TEACHER
OF THE
YEAR AWARD

George and Harold watched impatiently while Wedgie Woman's hair assembled thousands of assorted screws, bolts, wires, gears, cathode tubes, and computer chips. Soon, two small robots began taking shape.

"I didn't know Ms. Ribble was smart enough to make robots," said Harold.

"Me, neither," said George. "I think some of that Extra-Strength Super Power Juice must have soaked into her *brain*!"

The next morning, Wedgie Woman completed her robots, which she named "Robo-George" and "The Harold 2000."

"You know," said Harold, "something about those robots seems a little *familiar*!"

"Yeah," said George. "They kinda look like us . . . only not as dashingly handsome."

Wedgie Woman opened the robots' chest plates and inserted a can of spray starch into each one. Then she sealed the chest plates, patted each robot on the head, and sent them both off to school. "Captain Underpants doesn't stand a chance now!" Wedgie Woman laughed.

"Wait a minute," said Harold. "How are those two robots going to stop Captain Underpants?"

"All they have to do is wait and listen," said Wedgie Woman. "And as soon as they hear the words 'Tra-La-Laaaaa!', *it'll all be over!*"

CHAPTER 18
ROBO-GEORGE AND
THE HAROLD 2000

"Uh, attention boys and girls," said Mr. Krupp
to the fourth graders. "Your teacher, Ms.
Ribble, didn't come to school today."

"Hooray!" shouted the children.

"*Settle down!*" Mr. Krupp shouted. "You're
still going to have all your classes!"

"Aww, *maaaan!*" moaned the children.

"But you're going to have a substitute
teacher," said Mr. Krupp.

"Hooray!" shouted the children.

"And it's going to be *me!*" said Mr. Krupp.

"Aww, *maaaan!*" moaned the children.

The whole day was pretty much like a normal day, except for one thing: Mr. Krupp couldn't understand why George and Harold were so well behaved.

They didn't make funny noises during science class, they didn't stick crayons up their noses during art class, and they didn't draw comic books during math class. In fact, they even walked past a sign without changing the letters around. Mr. Krupp was stunned.

"Alright, you two!" Mr. Krupp shouted. "I know you're up to something . . . You better stop being so good, or you're gonna be in *BIG TROUBLE!*"

TODAY'S LUNCH
GENETICALLY MODIFIED MEAT FLAVORED BEEF
WITH EXTRA BOVINE GROWTH HORMONES

But Robo-George and the Harold 2000 kept right on behaving. The only time they did something even remotely wrong was during recess. Everybody was playing kickball, and when it was the Harold 2000's turn to kick the ball, he kicked it pretty darn hard.

KA-BOINGGG!

The kickball tore right through the top
of page 101 and out the other side as it
sailed toward the outer regions of Earth's
atmosphere. Soon it broke free of our planet's
gravitational pull and began heading straight
toward the planet Uranus.

"A-HA!" shouted Mr. Krupp, as he pulled
out the official school rulebook and read
Rule #411 out loud: *It is against the rules
to kick school property into outer space!*
You're in trouble now, bub!"

But the Harold 2000 ignored Mr. Krupp and began running around the bases.

"Hey! I'm talking to you, Hutchins!" Mr. Krupp shouted. He pointed at the Harold 2000 and snapped his fingers.

SNAP!

Suddenly, Mr. Krupp began to change.
A silly-looking smile stretched across his
face, and he stood before the fourth graders
looking quite heroic. Quickly, he turned
and ran back into the school.

CHAPTER 19
TRA-LA-LUUUNATICS

Several minutes later, Captain Underpants flew out of Mr. Krupp's office window. As the hero zipped across the sky, he let out a triumphant "Tra-La-Laaaaa!"

When Robo-George and the Harold 2000 heard the words "Tra-La-Laaaaa!", they immediately stopped playing kickball. Suddenly, their arms began to extend and their legs stretched toward the sky.

Strange secret compartments in their ever-growing torsos opened up, revealing giant rocket boosters and the latest in advanced aviation technology. Steel panels on their faces and bodies expanded wildly as their complex structures swelled to highly improbable proportions.

Suddenly, flames shot out of their retro-thrusters as their bodies rose into the air. In no time at all, two gigantic robots were flying in hot pursuit of the Amazing Captain Underpants.

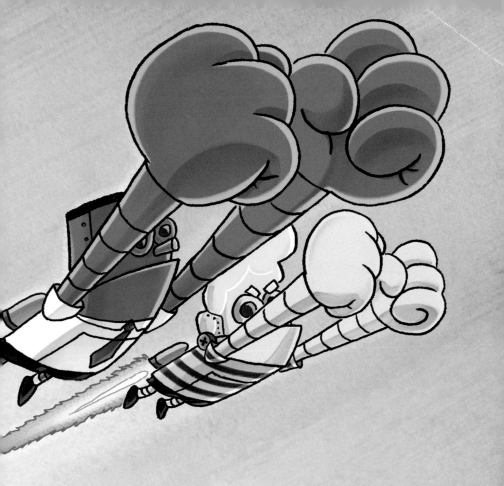

"George and Harold are in BIG trouble now," said Melvin Sneedly, as he read Rule #7,734 of Mr. Krupp's official school rulebook out loud: *"It is against the rules for students to transform into giant flying robots during afternoon recess!"*

The *real* George and Harold, however, had more on their minds at that moment than a few broken rules. They watched the action unfold on a big-screen television that Wedgie Woman's horrible hair had built by combining the spare parts of a fish tank and an electric toothbrush.

The colossal robots surrounded Captain Underpants, but surprisingly, the Waistband Warrior looked happy to see them.

"George! Harold!" said Captain Underpants. "My, how you boys have grown! And I didn't know you could fly. That's great! Now you can help me fight for Truth, Justice, and all that is Pre-Shrunk and Cottony!"

LIVE 4

But the gigantic robots didn't respond.
Instead, they hovered close to Captain
Underpants as their steel chest plates opened
up. Suddenly, two extendable robotic arms
reached out and began showering Captain
Underpants with liquid spray starch.

"What—what are you doing?" cried
Captain Underpants. "That's *SPRAY STARCH*!
It's the only thing in the world that can take
away my super powers!!!"

109

The Waistband Warrior screamed in
horror as he began falling through the
sky. Robo-George quickly swooped down,
grabbed the helpless hero, and hung him
by his waistband on a tall pole high above
the city streets.

CHAPTER 20
YOU AXED FOR IT

"Hooray!" cried Wedgie Woman as she turned off her new TV. "My plan worked. Now it's time to take over the world!"

"But what about us?" asked Harold.

"Don't worry," said Wedgie Woman. "I've got a big surprise for you two." She took a heavy battle-axe and tied it up with a rope. Then she leaned the axe toward George and Harold and lit a candle under the rope.

"When the flame burns through the rope," said Wedgie Woman, "all your problems will be over. Get the point?"

"Not really," said George.

"Don't worry," laughed Wedgie Woman. "You will soon enough."

Wedgie Woman laughed a horrible laugh. Then she dashed out the door to take on the world!

George and Harold watched as the flame began burning through the rope. They cringed as the impending doom of the axe blade came closer and closer.

"Well," said George, "it looks like this is the end."

"Maybe not," said Harold. "Maybe the blade will fall and slice through our ropes and not harm us at all."

"I doubt it," said George. "That kind of thing only happens in really lame adventure stories."

Suddenly, the blade fell and sliced through the ropes, not harming George or Harold at all. The two boys looked at each other and decided it was best not to comment on the situation.

CHAPTER 21
THE WOOTHLESS
WEVENGE OF THE WICKED
WEDGIE WOMAN

Wedgie Woman headed to the center of town
to meet up with Robo-George and the Harold
2000. "Well done, my precious robots," said
Wedgie Woman affectionately.

"What's all this then?" said a policeman
who had just arrived on the scene.

"Er—nothing, officer," said Wedgie Woman. "Just the beginning of my TOTAL WORLD DOMINATION!"

"Oh, OK," said the cop. "Hey, *wait a minute!*" But before the police officer could voice his objections, a twisted strand from Wedgie Woman's head shot out and grabbed the cop by the back of his underwear.

The colossal Harold 2000 lifted the officer and hung him from a stop sign. "Owie, *WOWIE*!" cried the cop.

Soon more police officers headed to the scene, but they all met with the same terrible fate as the first policeman.

Before long, every cop in the city
was hanging from a street sign.

"Call the National Guard!" screamed
the Chief of Police. "Call the Army —
call the Marines — call a *HAIRSTYLIST*!"

Soon, the armed forces arrived with a whole fleet of tanks and helicopters. But everybody was afraid to shoot. Wedgie Woman was just too quick.

The giant robots stomped around the city as Wedgie Woman barked out her commands. "Everybody on Earth must obey ME!" cried the Wicked Wedgie Woman. "If anybody refuses, they'll get the WEDGE! If anybody tries to stop me, it's WEDGIE TIME! Bow down to me . . . or *WELCOME TO WEDGIEVILLE*!"

Soon George and Harold arrived at the scene. They hid in some bushes and watched the terror unfold.

"We've got to rescue Captain Underpants," whispered George. "He's the only one who can save the world!"

"But how?" whispered Harold. "He's got no super powers left!"

"Sure he does!" said George. "Starch doesn't really take away super powers . . . he just *THINKS* it does. We've got to change his mind!"

"I sure hope we can!" said Harold.

CHAPTER 22
THEY CAN'T

George and Harold ran to the pole where the heartbroken hero was hanging.

"Hey, Captain Underpants," cried Harold. "You've got to come down from there and save the city!"

"C-Can't," whined the Waistband Warrior. "N-Need fabric softener!"

"No you *don't* need fabric softener!" said George sternly. "That was just a dumb joke in one of our comics!"

"But you don't understand," said Captain Underpants. "Starch is the enemy of underwear. Only fabric softener can save me!"

"*RATS!*" said Harold in frustration. "Hey, George, are there any stores around here?"

"Yeah," said George. "A new one just opened down on Oak Street."

"Then let's go buy some fabric softener," said Harold. "It'll be easier than trying to reason with the guy."

"How's that going to help?" asked George.

"It's all in his mind," Harold explained. "If he *believes* that fabric softener will save him, then it probably will. I think it's called 'the Placenta Effect.'"

So George and Harold ran to Oak Street. "What's the name of that store?" asked Harold.

"I can't remember," said George. "I think it's called 'Everything Except . . . umm —'"

"Aww, *maaaan!*" said George.

"We're doomed!" cried Harold.

"Listen," said George, "we've got
to make another comic book!"

"Now?!!?" asked Harold.

"It's our only hope," said George. "The fate of the entire planet is in our hands!" So the two boys bought some paper and a few pencils, and got down to work.

Twenty-two minutes later, George and Harold had created an all-new Captain Underpants adventure. They ran back to the pole where Captain Underpants was hanging and tossed their new comic up to him.

"This is no time to be reading comics," said Captain Underpants.

"Just read it, bub!" said Harold.

"Yeah," said George. "You might learn something!"

CHAPTER 23
THE ORIGIN OF
CAPTAIN UNDERPANTS

THE TRUE **UNTOLD** STORY!

By George Beard
and
Harold Hutchins

THE ORIJIN OF CAPTAin UnderPants

the TRUE UntoLD STORY By G. BEard and H. Hutchins

A far time Ago in a Galaxy Long, Long Away...

...there WAS A planet Called Underpantyworld.

Underpantyworld waS A peaseful planet where everybody wore only Underwear.

HA HA I can see your underwear.

Hey What are you doing under there?

Under where?

I can see yours to. Ha Ha Ha

Ha Ha You Said "Underwear"

Ha Ha

EveryBody Liked wearing Underwear so much that they never got into Fights and they dident have no wars either. It was Cool.

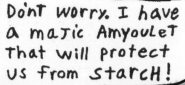

Don't worry. I have a majic Amyoulet that will protect us from starch!

Yipee!

But he Acksidentelly dropped the majic Amyoulet.

oopsies.

It fell into the mouth of his newborn Son, "Little Baby Underpants."

GULP.

OH NO-- He Swallowed it! we're Are Doomed

Just then the Wedgie Warlords sprayed starch on Underpantyworld.

WW

Starch ship Enterprize

Ssssssssss

BiG Daddy LongJohns and his Lovely wife "princess Pantyhose" knew that There planet WAS A goner. So They desided to SAVE There baby.

So they stretched his underwear REAL far.

Then one ~~day~~ night he had a weird dream.

SSSSS

He saw his old planet and his other parents.

Hi son Hows it Going?

Son, You aren't like other people. You are a super hero guy.

Also, You have a majical Amyoulet inside you. It will Protect you from The evils of starch!

All you half to do is say These words: "I SUMMON THE POWER OF UNDERPANTYWORLD." And you will overcome the powers of starch!

OK

So Captain Awoke up And Became a cool super hero guy....

CHAPTER 24
THE PLACENTA EFFECT

"Wow," said Captain Underpants. "I didn't realize that I had the power within me all along to overcome the evils of starch."

"JUST SAY THE WORDS!" shouted George and Harold.

"OK," said Captain Underpants. "But I think it's a great metaphor for —"

"JUST SAY THE WORDS!" yelled George and Harold.

"*Alright!*" said Captain Underpants. "But all I'm saying is that—"

"*JUST SAY THE WORDS!*" screamed George and Harold.

"You know," said Captain Underpants, "you kids have *NO* feel for dramatic tension!" Then he cleared his throat and spoke in a powerful voice. "I SUMMON THE POWER OF UNDERPANTYWORLD!" Suddenly, Captain Underpants rose triumphantly into the air. He was free at last!

When the gigantic robots saw that Captain Underpants had escaped, the Harold 2000 launched its rocket arms at our hero.

Captain Underpants grabbed the giant robo-arms and swung them around toward his foes.

"These might come in handy," said the Waistband Warrior.

CHAPTER 25
THE INCREDIBLY GRAPHIC VIOLENCE CHAPTER (IN FLIP-O-RAMA™)

WARNING:

The following chapter contains scenes that are so violent and naughty, you aren't allowed to view them.

We're not kidding.

DO NOT READ THE FOLLOWING CHAPTER!

Don't even look at it. Just skip ahead to page 156, and don't ask any questions.

P.S. Don't breathe on it, either.

PILKEY® BRAND
D-RAMA

HERE'S HOW IT WORKS!

STEP 1
First, give yourself eleven spankings and one time-out. Then, place your *left* hand inside the dotted lines marked "LEFT HAND HERE." Hold the book open *flat*.

STEP 2
Grasp the *right-hand* page with your right thumb and index finger (inside the dotted lines marked "RIGHT THUMB HERE").

STEP 3
Now *quickly* flip the right-hand page back and forth until the picture appears to be *animated*.

(For extra fun, try adding your own sound-effects!)

FLIP-O-RAMA 1

(pages 141 and 143)

Remember, flip *only* page 141.
While you are flipping, be sure you
can see the picture on page 141
and the one on page 143.
If you flip quickly, the two
pictures will start to look like
<u>one</u> *animated* picture.

Don't forget to
add your own sound-effects!

LEFT HAND HERE

ROUGHIN' UP
ROBO-GEORGE

RIGHT
THUMB
HERE

RIGHT
INDEX
FINGER
HERE

ROUGHIN' UP
ROBO-GEORGE

FLIP-O-RAMA 2

(pages 145 and 147)

Remember, flip *only* page 145.
While you are flipping, be sure you
can see the picture on page 145
and the one on page 147.
If you flip quickly, the two
pictures will start to look like
<u>one</u> *animated* picture.

Don't forget to
add your own sound-effects!

LEFT HAND HERE

HORRIBLY HURTIN' THE HAROLD 2000

RIGHT
INDEX
FINGER
HERE

HORRIBLY HURTIN'
THE HAROLD 2000

FLIP-O-RAMA 3

(pages 149 and 151)

Remember, flip *only* page 149.
While you are flipping, be sure you
can see the picture on page 149
and the one on page 151.
If you flip quickly, the two
pictures will start to look like
<u>one</u> *animated* picture.

Don't forget to
add your own sound-effects!

LEFT HAND HERE

LET'S PUT OUR HEADS TOGETHER!

RIGHT THUMB HERE

RIGHT
INDEX
FINGER
HERE

150

LET'S PUT OUR
HEADS TOGETHER!

FLIP-O-RAMA 4

(pages 153 and 155)

Remember, flip *only* page 153.
While you are flipping, be sure you
can see the picture on page 153
and the one on page 155.
If you flip quickly, the two
pictures will start to look like
<u>one</u> *animated* picture.

Don't forget to
add your own sound-effects!

LEFT HAND HERE

THE SUPER-SMASHY
CYBER SLAM

RIGHT
THUMB
HERE

RIGHT
INDEX
FINGER
HERE

154

THE SUPER-SMASHY
CYBER SLAM

156

CHAPTER 26
REVERSE PSYCHOLOGY 2

The giant robots were defeated, but the battle was not over yet. Harold ran back to their tree house to grab the 3-D Hypno-Ring, while George ran back to Everything Except Fabric Softener for some more supplies.

Soon George returned to the center of town carrying a big cardboard box filled with spray cans.

"What are you doing with that?" asked Harold, who had just arrived with the 3-D Hypno-Ring.

"I'm taking this *Extra-Strength Spray Starch* someplace where Wedgie Woman won't be able to find it!" George shouted rather loudly.

"*Extra-Strength Spray Starch?*" cried the Wicked Wedgie Woman. "That's just what I need!" Her winding hair lashed out at George, stopping him dead in his tracks. Then nine twisting braids each grabbed a can from the box and began spraying them at Captain Underpants.

A huge cloud of mist filled
the air, covering everything in
sight, and making these two
pages incredibly easy to draw.

When the cloud finally lifted, all of Wedgie Woman's hair was gone. In fact, all of EVERYBODY'S hair was gone.

"See?" George explained. "There was no spray starch in this box. This box was just a cleverly disguised carton of hair remover. I used *reverse psychology* on her."

"Aaugh!" screamed Harold, as he clutched his bald head. "My mom's gonna lay hard-boiled eggs when she sees me!"

"Relax," said George. "Our hair will grow back!"

"That's easy for you to say," said Harold. "Your hair was only half an inch long!"

CHAPTER 27
REVERSE REVERSE PSYCHOLOGY

"Well, Wedgie Woman," said Captain Underpants. "It's off to jail with you!"

"Wait a second," said Harold. "We'll take care of Wedgie Woman. You go back to the school, put some clothes on, then wash your face."

"Yeah, bub," said George. "Use plenty of water! We've got work to do."

"OK," said Captain Underpants.

So Captain Underpants did as he was told, and in no time at all he was back to his Kruppy old self. It was now time to transform Wedgie Woman back to her old self, too . . . *with some slight modifications.*

"OK," said Harold, "remember when we hypnotized Ms. Ribble, and she did the opposite of everything we wanted her to do?"

"Yeah," said George.

"Well, if we want to set things right," Harold continued, "we've got to hypnotize her into doing the *opposite* of the opposite of what we want."

"I'm way ahead of you," said George.

So the two boys once again hypnotized their teacher. Only this time, they used reverse *reverse* psychology on her.

"From now on," said George, "you will ALWAYS be known as Wedgie Woman."

"You WILL keep all your super powers, too," said Harold.

"You WILL NOT go back to teaching fourth grade," said George.

"You WILL remember everything that happened in the last two weeks," said Harold.

"You WILL NOT change our grades back to normal," said George.

"You WILL NOT become the nicest teacher in the history of Jerome Horwitz Elementary School," said Harold.

"And you WILL NOT bake fresh chocolate chip cookies for our class every day," said George.

"George!" said Harold sternly. "Stop goofing around!"

"I can't help it," said George. "You should never hypnotize anybody when you're hungry!"

"OK, OK," said Harold. "Let's just snap our fingers and PRAY that this works."

SNAP!

CHAPTER 28
TO MAKE A LONG
STORY SHORT

It did.

CHAPTER 29

BETTER LIVING THROUGH HYPNOSIS

The next day, Ms. Ribble entered the classroom looking a whole lot friendlier than usual.

"Boys and girls," said Ms. Ribble, "I have some good news for you."

"Hooray!" cried the children.

"It's time for English class," said Ms. Ribble.

"Aww, *maaaan*," moaned the children.

"Today," said Ms. Ribble, "I've asked George and Harold to lead the class."

"Hooray!" cried the children.

"They're going to teach us about creative writing . . ." said Ms. Ribble.

"Aww, *maaaan*," moaned the children.

". . . by showing us how to make our own comic books!" said Ms. Ribble.

"Hooray!" cried the children.

"While they're doing that," said Ms. Ribble, "I'm going to pass out something for you all to work on . . ."

"Aww, *maaaan*," moaned the children.

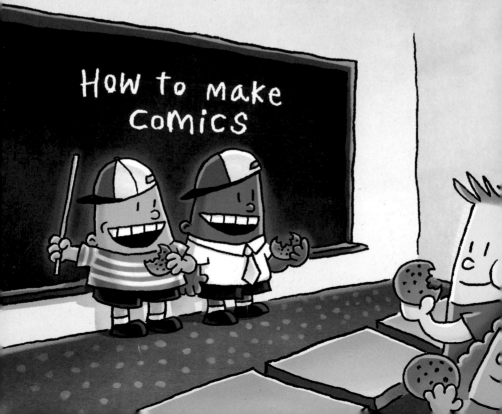

". . . Homemade chocolate chip cookies!" said Ms. Ribble.

"Hooray!" cried the children.

"This is awesome," said Harold, "but do you think it was right for us to change her personality like we did?"

"Sure, why not?" said George. "She's happier. She'll probably live longer!"

"You're right," said Harold. "I guess hypnosis is a pretty cool thing sometimes."

Then again (as we all know) sometimes it isn't.

"OH, NO!" screamed Harold.
"Here we go again!" screamed George.

FULL COLOUR
CAPTAIN UNDERPANTS
AND THE BIG, BAD BATTLE OF THE BIONIC BOOGER BOY
PART 1: THE NIGHT OF THE NASTY NOSTRIL NUGGETS

The Sixth Epic Novel by
DAV PILKEY

with color by Jose Garibaldi

SCHOLASTIC

For Amy Berkower and Jodi Reamer

CHAPTERS

FOREWORD:
The Awful Truth About Captain Underpants   183

1. George and Harold   187

2. Squishies, Part 1   193

3. The Combine-O-Tron 2000   200

4. Bad Sulu   210

5. The Incredibly Graphic Violence Chapter,
   Part 1 (in Flip-O-Rama™)   213

6. The Aftermath   220

7. Mr. Krupp   223

8. The Comic Is Mightier Than the Spitball   231

9. Captain Underpants and the Terrifying
   Tale of the Tattle-Tron 2000   237

10. Mad Mr. Melvin   247

11. Melvin's Fantasy   252

12. The Night of the Nasty Nostril Nuggets   256

13. The Next Day   260

14. The Unnecessarily Disgusting Chapter   265

15. The New Melvin   272

16. The Cold and Flu Season   277

17. The Field Trip   283

18. Things Get Bad   286

19. Things Get Badder   291

20. Captain Underpants, That's Who   300

21. You Can't Have Your Cape and Edith, Too   306

22. Welcome Back, Krupper   313

23. Sulu Saves the Day   317

24. The Incredibly Graphic Violence Chapter,
    Part 2 (in Flip-O-Rama™)   321

25. How to Reverse the Effects of a
    Combine-O-Tron 2000 in One Easy Step   334

26. *BLAZZZZT!*   338

27. To Make a Long Story Short   342

28. A Happy Ending   343

George and Harold Proudly Present

THE AWFUL TRUTH ABOUT CAPTAIN UNDERPANTS

A Treehouse Comix Production

Onse upon a time there was two cool kids named George and Harold.

We Da man!

me too.

They had a mean old prin-sipel named Mr. Krupp.

GRRRR

Hey Bubs!

Blah Blah Blah

One time Mr. Krupp punished George and Harold.

You half To oBey my orders

So they got a 3-D Hypno Ring and Hypnotised him.

No way! you must obey us now

ok.

Nowadays,
Whenever mr.
Krupp hears
anybody snap
there fingers...

Snap

...He turns
into you-know-
who!

Tra-La-Laaaa!

UH OH

NoT again

And the only
way you can
stop him is if
you pore water
on his head.

H2O

what the?

Then he Turns
Back into
Mr. Krupp.

Hey Whats the
Big idea
Bubs?

So whatever you do, Dont snap
your fingers around mr. krupp ok?

THE END

CHAPTER 1
GEORGE AND HAROLD

This is George Beard and Harold Hutchins.
George is the kid on the left with the tie
and the flat-top. Harold is the one on the
right with the T-shirt and the bad haircut.
Remember that now.

George's and Harold's grades in school were much like whales in the ocean: They rarely rose above "C" level.

Melvin Sneedly, however (he's the kid down there with the bow tie and the glasses), always got straight As.

Because Melvin was so academically gifted, people just assumed he was a lot smarter than George and Harold.

But that wasn't true.

You see, George and Harold were every bit as smart as the *straight A* students . . . but in a *different* way. In a way that couldn't be measured by quizzes or worksheets.

Maybe George and Harold couldn't spell very well or remember their multiplication tables. Perhaps their grammar weren't no good neither. But when it came to saving the entire planet from the nasty forces of unrelenting evil, there was nobody better than George Beard and Harold Hutchins.

It's a good thing that George and Harold were smart enough to get themselves out of trouble, because their silliness was always getting them *into* trouble. In fact, one time it got them into a really *SNOTTY* situation.

But before I can tell you that story, I have to tell you *this* story . . .

CHAPTER 2
SQUISHIES, PART 1

It was Demonstration Speech Day in Ms. Ribble's fourth-grade English class. Every student had to give an oral report demonstrating how to do something. First up were Tim Bronski and Stevie Loopner, who demonstrated how to give a speech that they hadn't prepared for.

They got a D-.

Next up were Jessica Gordon and Stephanie Wycoff, who demonstrated how to cook frozen lasagna in a pop-up toaster.

After the firemen left, it was George and Harold's turn. Harold carefully tacked some charts and graphs onto the wall while George brought out a large garbage can with a toilet seat taped to the top.

SIDE VEIW

SQUISHIES

① ketchup ② ketchup ↖ ③

CROSS Seckshon

seat

← BUMPY Thingy

← kechup

← Bowl

SIDE Veiw

"Ladies and gentlemen," said George. "Today Harold and I are going to demonstrate how to do a Squishy. First, you need two packets of ketchup and a toilet seat."

"Next," said Harold as he pointed to their display chart, "you must fold the ketchup packets in half and carefully place them under the toilet seat. Make sure that the packets are under those front two bumpy thingies on the bottom of the seat."

"Now, once the ketchup packets are in place," said Harold, "all you have to do is wait for somebody to sit down on the toilet seat. Do we have any volunteers?"

"C'mon," said George, "who wants a Squishy?"

Although nobody in the class wanted to sit on the toilet seat, everybody wanted to see what would happen if somebody actually DID. So George grasped one side of the toilet seat, Harold grasped the other, and together they pushed down.

SPLAT!!! SPLAT!!!

Everyone in the class was thrilled
(except for the two kids sitting directly in
front of the toilet seat, who were somewhat
less-than-thrilled). "Hooray for Squishies!"
the children shouted.

Now, normally George and Harold's
teacher, Ms. Ribble, would have been very
angry about this particular demonstration
speech.

She would have yelled on and on about "imitateable behavior" and how it's not nice to spray ketchup into people's underwear. But Ms. Ribble had changed quite a bit since the last book, and now she was all about FUN!

"C'mon, kids," shouted Ms. Ribble. "Let's all run to the cafeteria and grab some ketchup packets! Squishies for EVERYBODY!!!"

"HOORAY!" cried the children as they bounded from their seats and dashed toward the classroom door.

"NOT SO FAST!" shouted Melvin Sneedly, who stood blocking the door with his arms spread defiantly. "You guys are _so_ immature!"

CHAPTER 3
THE COMBINE-O-TRON 2000

Melvin Sneedly, the school brainiac, was not
about to let anybody leave the classroom
until he had given his demonstration speech.

"We still have fifteen minutes left before
lunch," said Melvin, "and that's just enough
time for me to demonstrate my new
invention, the Combine-O-Tron 2000."

"Aww, *maaaan*!" whined Melvin's
classmates.

The children all slumped back into their seats while Melvin pushed a plastic rolling cart to the front of the classroom. On top of the cart were a hamster, a small robot (which Melvin had built himself), and a strange-looking contraption shaped like an ice-cream cone.

"Today," said Melvin, "I will demonstrate how to turn an ordinary hamster into your very own bionic cyber-servant."

Melvin placed his pet hamster, Sulu, at one end of the cart, and his tiny homemade robot at the other end. "I shall now combine this ordinary hamster with this tiny robot using the Combine-O-Tron 2000."

Melvin picked up the Combine-O-Tron 2000 and turned it on. A high-pitched tone pierced the classroom air, getting higher and higher in frequency as the machine charged to full power. Melvin typed some last-minute calculations into the keyboard on the side of the Combine-O-Tron 2000 as its laser extractor warmed up.

Suddenly, two streaks of red glowing light flashed onto Sulu and the tiny robot. The Combine-O-Tron 2000 began assimilating information on the two elements it was about to combine. "Don't worry, kids," said Melvin. "This procedure is totally painless. Sulu won't feel a thing." Finally, a computerized voice started the countdown:

"Combining two elements in five seconds.
Combining two elements in four seconds.
Combining two elements in three seconds.
Combining two elements in two seconds.
Combining two elements in one second."

BLAZZZZT!

A burst of brilliant white light shot out
of the Combine-O-Tron 2000 and formed a
ball of energy between Sulu and the tiny
robot. The hamster and the robot began to
slide closer and closer together until they
disappeared into the energy ball.

The smell of burned matches and pickle relish filled the air as hot blasts of electric wind knocked books off of shelves and sent papers flying. Suddenly, there was a blinding flash of light, a quick puff of smoke, and it was all over.

Melvin pulled off his goggles. No longer were a hamster and a robot sitting on the cart before him. Now the hamster and robot were one, combined at a cellular level. The world's first self-contained, warm-blooded, fuzzy bionic cyborg.

"EUREKA!" shouted Melvin. "IT WORKED! I have created a cybernetic life-form."

The children looked on as Melvin waved a metal detector over the hamster and the reading went off the chart. One of the children raised his hand with a question.

"Yes!" said Melvin enthusiastically.

"Can we go to the lunchroom and get our ketchup packets now?"

"Bu —NO!" screamed Melvin. "Will you forget about Squishies for ONE MINUTE?!!? I've just created the world's first cybernetic hamster, and nobody is leaving this room until I've demonstrated his undying obedience!"

CHAPTER 4
BAD SULU

Sulu didn't seem to know that he had just undergone a groundbreaking transformation. He didn't act any different. He just wandered across the top of the plastic rolling cart sniffing everything around him, only stopping occasionally to scratch his ears or rub his whiskers. But poor Sulu was in for a big surprise.

"Sulu," said Melvin, "I am your commander, and you will obey my orders. I want you to demonstrate your new powers for the class. Do a super-bionic jump across the room."

Sulu did not respond.

SNIFF
SNIFF

"Sulu!" said Melvin sternly. "Crush that
plastic rolling cart in your bare paws!"

Sulu did not respond.

"SULU!" Melvin shouted. "Go outside, pick
up a car, and throw it across the parking lot!"

Sulu did not respond.

Finally, Melvin reached into his book bag
and took out a red Ping-Pong paddle he had
designed especially for this occasion. "Sulu,"
he said angrily, "do as I say, or you're going
to get a good spanking!"

This time, Sulu did
respond. When he saw the Ping-Pong paddle
he became very frightened, and his little
hamster instincts took over. Sulu jumped
into the air, grabbed the Ping-Pong paddle in
his right paw, and then yanked Melvin onto
the plastic rolling cart with his left paw.

The children finally stopped thinking
about ketchup packets and toilets for a
moment and settled in to watch the show.

CHAPTER 5
THE INCREDIBLY GRAPHIC VIOLENCE CHAPTER, PART 1 (IN FLIP-O-RAMA™)

WARNING:

The following chapter contains graphic depictions of a mean little boy getting spanked by a bionic hamster. While this event is presented for humorous effect, the producers of this book acknowledge that hamster attacks are no laughing matter. If you or someone you love has been the victim of a hamster attack, we strongly urge you to get help by seeking out a local support group in your area, or by visiting www.whenhamstersattack.com.

PILKEY® BRAND

C.RAMA

HERE'S HOW IT WORKS!

STEP 1
First, place your *left* hand inside the dotted lines marked "LEFT HAND HERE." Hold the book open *flat*.

STEP 2
Grasp the *right-hand* page with your right thumb and index finger (inside the dotted lines marked "RIGHT THUMB HERE").

STEP 3
Now *quickly* flip the right-hand page back and forth until the picture appears to be *animated*.

(For extra fun, try adding your own sound-effects!)

FLIP-O-RAMA 1

(pages 217 and 219)

Remember, flip *only* page 217.
While you are flipping, be sure you
can see the picture on page 217
and the one on page 219.
If you flip quickly, the two
pictures will start to look like
<u>one</u> *animated* picture.

Don't forget to
add your own sound-effects!

LEFT HAND HERE

SPANKS FOR THE MEMORIES.

RIGHT
THUMB
HERE

RIGHT
INDEX
FINGER
HERE

218

SPANKS FOR THE
MEMORIES.

CHAPTER 6
THE AFTERMATH

Although Sulu hadn't *really* spanked Melvin
very hard, Melvin wailed and blubbered and
carried on anyway.

"You're a BAD hamster!" Melvin cried. "I
never want to see you again as long as I live!"

Melvin ran out of the classroom sobbing. The rest of the class, including Ms. Ribble, followed him out laughing and chanting, "Squish-ies, Squish-ies, Squish-ies!" But George and Harold stayed behind to comfort the forgotten hamster.

"Don't feel bad, Sulu," said George. "Melvin is a real meanie!"

"Yeah," said Harold. "Do you want to come home with us? You can live up in our tree house."

Sulu jumped into Harold's arms and
gave him a hug. Then he jumped into
George's arms and hugged him, too.

"I think we've just adopted a bionic
hamster," said Harold.

So George tucked their new pal into his
shirt pocket, and the three friends went
off to lunch.

CHAPTER 7
MR. KRUPP

About that very same time, the school principal, Mr. Krupp, came marching into the office in a particularly foul mood. He stopped beside Miss Anthrope's desk, huffing and puffing.

"Where's my coffee, Edith?" he shouted.

"Get it yourself!" Miss Anthrope shouted back.

"I don't need your lip today!" Mr. Krupp growled. "I just want my coffee and I want it NOW!"

"Well, get me a cup, too, while you're at it," Miss Anthrope growled back.

"Aaaaugh!" screamed Mr. Krupp in frustration as he grabbed a newspaper and headed for the faculty restroom. Ms. Ribble was standing beside the restroom door smiling and trying very hard not to laugh.

"What are *you* lookin' at?" Mr. Krupp snarled as he pushed his way past Ms. Ribble and slammed the restroom door behind him. Inside the restroom, you could hear the faint sound of a belt buckle jingling, a zipper unzipping, some clothes rustling, and finally . . .

SPLAT!!! SPLAT!!!

"WHAT THE—!" screamed Mr. Krupp
from inside the restroom. "I'VE GOT
KETCHUP IN MY UNDERWEAR!!!"

In a few moments, the door of the
faculty restroom flew open. "I'm going to
get George and Harold for this!" Mr. Krupp
screamed.

"They didn't do it," laughed Ms. Ribble. "I
did! It's called a *Squishy*. It's the latest fad!"

"Yeah, right. Very funny!" said Mr. Krupp.
"Now, where are those two kids? I just *KNOW*
they're responsible!"

As Mr. Krupp headed for the cafeteria, he noticed that he wasn't the only person to fall victim to the dreaded Squishies. All through the hallway, angry first, second, third, fifth, and sixth graders were complaining about ketchup stains on their pants, socks, legs, and underwear. Mr. Krupp stormed into the cafeteria and headed for the fourth graders' table.

"George and Harold!" shouted Mr. Krupp.
"I've got ketchup in my underwear because
of you two. And so do half of the kids in
this school!"

"We didn't do it," said Harold.

"Yeah," said a few of the other fourth
graders. "George and Harold are innocent."

"Oh, no they're NOT," said a voice from
the other end of the table. It was Melvin
Sneedly. Besides being the school brainiac,
Melvin was also famous for being the school
tattletale. "George and Harold taught everybody
a trick today where you put ketchup packets
under a toilet seat and make it spray on
people's legs," Melvin reported proudly.

"Thank you, Melvin," said Mr. Krupp. He
turned to George and Harold and pointed at
the cafeteria door. "Mr. Beard and Mr.
Hutchins—OUT!"

CHAPTER 8
THE COMIC IS MIGHTIER
THAN THE SPITBALL

George and Harold were sent straight to
the detention room.

"Man," said Harold, "Melvin is such a
tattletale. Somebody ought to teach him
a lesson."

"And we're just the guys to do it,"
said George.

So George and Harold created an all-new comic book featuring everybody's favorite tattletalin' meanie, Melvin Sneedly. When they were done, the two boys sneaked out of the detention room to run off copies of their latest work and sell them in the hallway.

The new comic book was a great success. Everybody loved it. Well, everybody but Melvin Sneedly, I should say. As Melvin walked to his last class of the day, he noticed small groups of students in the hallway reading comics together and giggling. Normally, this was enough to make Melvin run straight to the principal's office and tell on everyone for unsupervised reading (which was strictly forbidden). But today, Melvin noticed something strange. The comic-reading students were pointing and laughing — at HIM.

"What?" said Melvin. "What's wrong? What
are you guys laughing at?" Melvin looked
around the hallway desperately. Everybody
was laughing . . . everybody was pointing . . .
and it was driving Melvin crazy! He marched
over to a group of second graders, grabbed
the comic book out of their hands, and
looked at the cover. Melvin was FURIOUS!

"YOU GUYS ARE _SO_ IMMATURE!!!"
shrieked Melvin. He quickly darted off to
read the comic in peace, but everywhere he
ran, he came across more pointing and more
laughing. Finally, Melvin thought of the one
place he could read the comic in private. He
went into the boys' bathroom, locked himself
in one of the stalls, and sat down to read.

SPLAT!!! SPLAT!!!

As Melvin sat reading, his legs dripping with ketchup, he became angrier and angrier. "I'm gonna get George and Harold!" Melvin vowed.

CHAPTER 9
CAPTAIN UNDERPANTS AND THE TERRIFYING TALE OF THE TATTLE-TRON 2000

CAPTAIN UNDERPANTS
AND THE TERIFYING TALE
OF THE TATTLE-TRON 2000

By George Beard and Harold Hutchins

Onse upon a time There was a dumb kid named Melvin who was a big Tattle-tale.

I'm Telling

KEEP OFF THE GRASS

Everywhare He went he caused Greif and Mizery.

Im Telling

NO SKATE BORDING

Until one Day...

BANK

I'm Telling

$

CRASH

Hey cops, That guy Just Robed the Bank.

Gee thanks Kid.

$

Soon mayer Melvin made a bunch of Dumb new Laws.

And People were getting aRested Left and Right

And they all got sent to Jail

Sudenly...

Mayer Melvin ALL THE JAILS are FULL!

Hmm

Mayer

I will Build a big Robo-Jail and catch those Lawbrakers myself!

So he built the Tattle-Tron 2000

CLANG CLANG

?

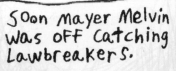

Soon Mayer Melvin was off catching lawbreakers.

NO oLd Ladies

That'll teach you!

Then Melvin Headed for the sckool.

Help! The Tattle-Tron 2000 Just Ran across the soccer Feild and sQuished the Gym Teacher!

OH NO! we just Planted that grass!

Prinsiple

This Looks Like a JOB FOR...

Prinsiple

CRASH

CAPTAIN UNDerPANts!

captain Underpants wanted to fight the Robot but he dident want to hurt the people inside.

Then he got a idea.

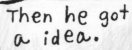

CRASH

mrs. Plops PRUNE JUICE FACKTERY

"It makes you go poop"

Hey!

Prune Juice

What the ???

UH-OH

Soon There was no-
Body Left inside
The Tattle-Tron 2000
Exsept For melvin.

CHAPTER 10
MAD MR. MELVIN

Melvin was furious. He ripped the comic book in half and tossed it over his shoulder. Then he washed his hands in the toilet and stormed out of the restroom.

"I'm gonna get George and Harold for that," said Melvin. "I'm gonna teach them a lesson they'll NEVER forget!"

After school, Melvin grabbed his Combine-O-Tron 2000 and headed home.

Melvin's mother and father were both busy working on a top-secret government experiment when Melvin walked in the front door.

"Hello, son," said Melvin's father. "How was your day at school?"

"Terrible!" said Melvin. "Nobody in school has sufficient respect for my beautiful mind. Those dull-witted, lame-brained, gum-chewing idiots are more impressed with comic books than they are with the wonders of science. But I shall teach them. I shall teach them all! Ha-ha-ha-ha-haaaa!"

"That's nice, honey," said Melvin's mom.

Melvin marched up to his room to begin building a brand-new super-powered robot. But when he opened his bedroom door, he saw the family's pet cat, Danderella, sleeping quietly on his bed.

"Hey!" Melvin screamed. "What are you doing in my room, you stupid cat? You know I'm allergic to you! Now get out and—a-a-A-CHOOO!—STAY OUT!"

After a few hours, Melvin had built his newest and most powerful robot ever, which had three sets of interchangeable laser eyeballs, Macro-Hydraulic Jump-A-Tronic legs, Super-Somgobulating Automo-Arms, and an extendable Octo-Claw rib cage, and was powered by three separate Twin Turbo-9000 SP5 Kung-Fu Titanium/Lithium Alloy Processors, which were all built into a virtually indestructible Flexo-Growmonic endoskeleton that had the power to punch through cinder blocks, crush steel in its vise-like grasp, and plow mercilessly through poorly written run-on sentences.

It could also slice bagels.

"That ought to do the trick," said Melvin, wiping his nose on a tissue. "Now, all I have to do is—a-a-A-Chooo!—combine my body with this bionic robot, and I shall be the most powerful boy who—a-a-A-Chooo!— ever lived!"

CHAPTER 11
MELVIN'S FANTASY

As Melvin set up the Combine-O-Tron 2000 and made the proper adjustments, he imagined what his life would be like as the world's first bionic boy. He imagined himself walking into school the next day, his arms swinging confidently as he crashed through the classroom wall.

The girls would swoon as Melvin talked for hours about the amazing world of science. Ms. Ribble would probably let Melvin sit at her desk from now on, because Melvin's new buns of steel would be too massive to fit into an ordinary children's chair.

Maybe Mr. Krupp would invite the governor to visit the school, so he could show off his smartest and most powerful student. If so, the governor would probably declare a new holiday, "National Melvin Sneedly Day": a day when kids all over the world would get extra homework and pop quizzes to honor the glorious name of Melvin.

But the best part of all would be George and Harold's reaction. They would be so terrified by Melvin's incredible size and strength, they'd drop to their knees and beg for mercy. And Melvin would spare them only if they agreed to be his servants for all eternity. They'd have to carry his books, sharpen his pencils, and be his personal footstools during each class.

"Life is gonna—a-a-A-Chooo!—RULE!" said Melvin.

CHAPTER 12
THE NIGHT OF THE NASTY NOSTRIL NUGGETS

Melvin turned on the Combine-O-Tron 2000. A high-pitched tone pierced the air, getting higher and higher in frequency as the machine charged to full power. "Oops," said Melvin as he quickly turned the Dramatic Effects setting to "off" so he wouldn't disturb his parents. Silently, the machine continued to charge as Melvin entered calculations to account for his clothes and glasses. When the laser extractor had finally warmed up, Melvin stepped in front of the Combine-O-Tron 2000, standing perfectly still beside his new robot.

Suddenly, two streaks of red glowing light flashed onto Melvin and the robot as the Combine-O-Tron 2000 began assimilating information on the two elements it was about to combine. Finally, a computerized voice started the countdown:

"**Combining two elements in five seconds.**"
Melvin stood perfectly still.
"**Combining two elements in four seconds.**"
Melvin's nose began to twitch.
"**Combining two elements in three seconds.**"
Suddenly, Melvin felt an uncontrollable urge. He cupped his hands over his mouth and nose as his eyes squeezed closed involuntarily. "A-a-a—"
"**Combining two elements in two seconds.**"

"—A-Chooo!" Melvin looked down into
his hands, which were now glistening with
mucus and crusty chunks of semi-dried
booglets. Instantly, the Combine-O-Tron
2000 began to recalculate the elements in its
laser sights.

"Combining three elements in one second."

"THREE elements?" Melvin screamed in horror. "W-W-What's the THIRD ELEMENT???"

Quickly, Melvin's eyes darted around the room, searching for any new element that might have accidentally made its way into the sights of the laser extractor.

"WHAT'S THE THIRD ELEMENT???" he screamed again. Then he looked down into his crusty, dripping, phlegm-filled hands.

"Uh-oh," said Melvin as a blinding burst of white light enveloped him.

BLAZZZZT!

CHAPTER 13
THE NEXT DAY

The next day, Melvin didn't show up for school on time. Nobody really seemed to notice, though, because all the children were excited about show-and-tell. Almost everyone had brought in really lame stuff like books or awards, but George and Harold had something that was totally *cool*.

"Everybody remembers Sulu from yesterday, right?" said George. "Well, we took him home to live with us in our tree house."

"And we taught him the greatest trick!" said Harold.

The two boys carried Sulu over to the classroom window and opened it up. Harold pulled a large watermelon out of his book bag and showed it to Sulu.

"OK, Sulu," said George, "show everybody your new trick!"

In one swift motion, Sulu placed his mouth onto the watermelon and shoved the entire thing into his left cheek. The fourth graders were stunned.

"No, no," said Harold, "that's not the trick. The trick is what happens next!"

Sulu looked out the window and eyed
a dead tree at the far end of the empty
playground. Sulu began to chew up the
watermelon, then puckered his tiny
hamster lips and spit.

Ratatatatatatatatatatatatatatat!

The watermelon seeds fired out of Sulu's mouth, hitting their target with expert precision. In no time at all, the dead tree at the end of the playground was reduced to a pile of twigs and sawdust. The class cheered as George and Harold petted their amazing little bionic buddy.

George and Harold didn't think that anybody could beat their show-and-tell display, but they were wrong. Because at that very moment, Melvin Sneedly was dripping down the hallway toward the classroom door. Melvin hadn't brought anything for show-and-tell. Melvin WAS the show-and-tell.

CHAPTER 14
THE UNNECESSARILY DISGUSTING CHAPTER

NOTICE:

The following chapter is extremely gross.

To avoid nausea, projectile vomiting, or other gastrointestinal unpleasantries, please refrain from eating for at least one hour before reading this chapter.

(You won't want to eat after reading it, let me assure you.)

All of the fourth graders were cheering and petting Sulu as the classroom door slowly opened. A greenish, glistening behemoth entered the room, filling the air with the sounds of grinding metal gears and wet, gooey, bursting bubbles. Some of the girls screamed. Some of the boys did, too.

"You guys are _so_ immature!" said the horrible beast.

At once, the children recognized the terrifying creature that stood before them.

"*MELVIN?!!?*" they cried.

"Yes, it's me," gurgled the wet, jiggling monster angrily. His eyes and nose were dripping with warm, greenish, custard-like mucus. His robotic arms were caked with massive globs of crispy, shimmering snot. And as he turned to close the classroom door behind him, part of his hand came off on the doorknob. It oozed slowly down the door, leaving behind a chunky trail of moist excretion.

Melvin squished and sloshed as he jiggled over to his chair. Each gooey footstep coated the floor with a foamy trail of slime, and everything he touched became wet and encrusted with warm, bubbling, syrupy phlegm.

When Melvin sat down, generous helpings of greenish, pudding-like goo slowly dribbled down the chair, collecting into creamy, gelatinous puddles beneath him. The puddles

themselves were slightly transparent and
speckled with thick, shimmering nose hairs and
dark red chunks of coagulated blood, which —

"*ALRIGHT ALREADY!*" yelled George to the
narrator. "Enough with the descriptions — you're
making us all sick!"

"Thank you, George," said Ms. Ribble.
"Now, Melvin, why don't you tell us all what
happened to you?"

"Well," said Melvin, "I tried to combine myself with a bionic robot last night, but I accidentally sneezed at the last second."

"So you got combined with a robot—and *boogers*?" asked George.

"Yeah," said Melvin. "But don't worry, I'm building a Separatron 1000, which will reverse the effects and turn me back into a boy again. It'll just take six months to finish."

"Six *MONTHS*?" said Harold.

"Hey, cellular separation is a highly complex procedure," said Melvin. "It's not like building a robot. It takes time!"

"You should try taking the batteries out of that Combine-O-Thingy and putting them in backward," suggested George. "That might reverse the effect."

Melvin rolled his thick, bubbling, crust-covered infrared eyeballs. "That's the dumbest thing I've ever heard!" he gurgled.

CHAPTER 15
THE NEW MELVIN

You might think that turning into a Bionic Booger Boy was the worst thing that could ever happen to a kid, but it wasn't all bad. Believe it or not, there was actually a positive side to being a lumbering loogie lad. For instance, Melvin now won every football game he played . . . because no one wanted to tackle him.

And when he served a volleyball, nobody
on the other team would dare to hit the
ball back.

Besides being the school's new sports star, there were other perks, too. Melvin never had to wait in line at the drinking fountain anymore. Now he had his own *personal* drinking fountain, because . . . well, would *you* use a drinking fountain after a Bionic Booger Boy had globbered all over it?

I didn't think so.

All of the special attention that Melvin was receiving made some of the other kids a little jealous. But not George and Harold. Considering the many evil villains that George and Harold had been battling all year, the two boys were just grateful that Melvin hadn't turned himself into a gigantic, terrifying beast with plans to destroy the earth.

"It could be a LOT worse," said Harold. "At least Melvin's not a terrifying evil villain."

"Yeah, you're right," said George. "I can't think of *anything* that could turn Melvin into a terrifying evil villain . . ."

CHAPTER 16
THE COLD AND
FLU SEASON

Soon it was autumn, and the new season brought with it many changes: crisp, chilly air; early morning frost; and bright, colorful leaves. But with the beauty of autumn came another change that wasn't quite so welcome: *the cold and flu season*.

All through Jerome Horwitz Elementary School, people were getting sick. The hallways were filled with runny noses, sneezing mouths, and aching bodies.

And unfortunately, one of those
noses, mouths, and bodies belonged to
Melvin Sneedly.

Every time Melvin sneezed, thousands
of tiny driblets shot out of his mouth,

spattering the chalkboard with a thin
layer of foamy, glistening, gunky-green,
tapioca-like mucus.

"Don't forget to cover your mouth,
Melvin, dear," said Ms. Ribble.

279

"Oh, sorry," said Melvin. "Sorry." He put his hand over his mouth and sneezed again. This time, the explosion of air from his stifled sneeze blew off large, wet globs of his body, which sprayed over the entire classroom.

It was as if somebody set off a giant firecracker inside a bucket of green paint. The warm, smelly goo smacked into people's hair, splattered onto their clothes, and seemed to drench every square inch of the room.

"On second thought, Melvin," said Ms. Ribble, *"don't* cover your mouth next time. Now, who wants a cookie?"

CHAPTER 17
THE FIELD TRIP

The next day, for some strange reason, Ms. Ribble was out sick with a cold. Mr. Krupp was filling in as the substitute teacher and, as usual, he was very angry.

"What the *heck* is going on in this room?" he yelled. "What's with all the raincoats and umbrellas?"

Then Melvin sneezed.

A few moments later, Mr. Krupp returned to the classroom with fresh clothes, a raincoat, and an umbrella. "Alright, everybody," he shouted. "Today is Field Trip Day. Miss Anthrope and I are taking you all to Snoddy Bros. Tissue Factory to see how blow-rags are made."

The word *tissue* made Melvin jump. "NO!" he cried in a panic. "ME NO LIKE TISSUES!"

An eerie silence fell over the classroom. Everybody looked at Melvin in shock.

"Did Melvin just say *me no like tissues*?" asked Harold.

"Yeah," said George. "I've never heard him misuse an objective pronoun before. Who does he think he is, *Frankenstein*?"

CHAPTER 18
THINGS GET BAD

In a few hours, the fourth graders were all
packed into a hot, stinky factory listening to
a boring speech about how trees are turned
into tissues . . . or something like that.
Nobody was paying attention, really, except
for Melvin Sneedly, who was terrified. His
whole body shook and shimmered as the tour
took them down the narrow walkways of the
noisy industrial plant.

DANGER

BORING
TOUR
AHEAD

Finally, the tour ended at the gift shop, where the plant manager, Mr. Snoddy, had a surprise for everybody.

"Behind this red curtain with black dots on it," said Mr. Snoddy, "is a free gift for each of you." Mr. Snoddy pulled back the curtain to reveal a pile of sample tissue packs. "Help yourselves," said Mr. Snoddy. "There's enough for everybody!"

"NOOOOO!" screamed Melvin. "ME NO LIKE TISSUES!"

"Oh, don't be silly," said Mr. Snoddy. "Everybody *loves* tissues. And our tissues are extra absorbent. They really help to wipe out phlegm and mucus!"

"NOOOOO!" screamed Melvin again. "TISSUES IS *BAD MAGIC*!"

"Nonsense," laughed Mr. Snoddy. He tossed a couple of sample tissue packs at Melvin. "Here you go, young man," he said. "Enjoy!"

The tissue packs flipped through the air and stuck onto Melvin's back. Melvin screamed. His eyes began to glow green as he beat his chest in anger. Suddenly, Melvin's shoulders started to bubble. His chest expanded. The Flexo-Growmonic steel in Melvin's endoskeleton flexed and grew. His neck and head widened, and his body swelled to a height of thirteen feet.

Melvin grabbed the tissue packs in his massive, dripping fingers and flung them to the ground. "DON'T MAKE ME ANGRY!" Melvin warned. "YOU NO LIKE ME WHEN I ANGRY!"

"Oops," said Mr. Snoddy. "You dropped your tissue packs, young fellow. Here's some more for you!" Mr. Snoddy grabbed two giant handfuls of sample tissue packs and tossed them at Melvin.

CHAPTER 19
THINGS GET BADDER

Frantically, Melvin swatted at the nine new tissue packs stuck to his upper torso as if they were a swarm of stinging bumblebees. He stomped his giant spiked feet and thrashed about violently as his hulking body doubled, then *tripled* in size. Melvin kicked and punched the walls of the gift shop as he let out a terrifying, bloodcurdling cry.

"There's no need to cry, little man,"
said Mr. Snoddy. "Here — have some more
tissues to dry those tears!" He tossed several
more sample tissue packs at Melvin. (As
you might have noticed by now, Mr. Snoddy
wasn't exactly the brightest bulb on the
Hanukkah tree.)

What happened next could only be described as chaos. Once again, Melvin's massive body tripled in size. By now, Melvin was roaring and kicking and knocking over giant machines. Children screamed and ran.

Mr. Snoddy thought it might help matters if he could just give Melvin some more tissues. But before he could, a drop of mucus the size of a bathtub dripped from Melvin's massive nose and splashed down on Mr. Snoddy, gluing him to the floor.

George and Harold hid behind the red curtain with black dots on it as Melvin crashed through the roof of the factory. Ear-piercing roars bellowed out of his gigantic, oozing mouth as he kicked down the walls of the factory and tossed heavy machinery into the parking lot. Mr. Krupp and Miss Anthrope tried their best to get the situation under control, but they weren't having much luck.

"Hey, bub," shouted Mr. Krupp, "I've had just about enough of your shenanigans!"

"You're gonna be spending the afternoon in detention if you don't settle down, young man!" shouted Miss Anthrope.

Suddenly, Melvin reached down and grabbed Miss Anthrope in his massive metal fist.

"HELP ME!" she screamed. "SOMEBODY SAVE ME!"

"Uh . . . ummm . . ." said Mr. Krupp nervously, "I'll — I'll go get some help!"

Mr. Krupp ran and hid with George and Harold behind the red curtain with black dots on it.

"Hey, I thought you were going to go get some help!" said Harold.

"Well, not *today*," said Mr. Krupp.

"You know," said George, "there's only one person who can help Miss Anthrope now."

"Who's that?" asked Mr. Krupp.

CHAPTER 20
CAPTAIN UNDERPANTS,
THAT'S WHO

As much as George and Harold hated to do it, they decided that it was time to send in Captain Underpants to save the day. George snapped his fingers. Suddenly, the terror and panic that Mr. Krupp had been experiencing completely vanished.

A wild, silly grin spread across his face as he leaped to his feet and ripped off his outer clothing and toupee. Mr. Krupp's transformation into Captain Underpants was almost complete. The only thing he was missing was a cape.

"Gee," he said, "I sure wish I could find a red curtain with black dots on it."

"Hey," said George as he pointed to the red curtain with black dots on it, "here's a red curtain with black dots on it."

"What a remarkably unexpected coincidence," said Captain Underpants as he grabbed the latest in a series of convoluted plot devices and tied it around his neck.

By this time, Melvin had stomped his way out of the factory and into the downtown area, leaving behind a twisted path of mucus-coated destruction. Captain Underpants flew into the air, following the trail of terror until he was face-to-face with the snot-spewing cyborg.

"I order you to stop," said Captain Underpants, "in the name of all that is Pre-Shrunk and Cottony!" Melvin did not listen.

Captain Underpants had no choice but to fight the boogery behemoth, but first he needed to save Miss Anthrope. Quickly, our hero flew to Edith's side, grabbed her hands, and pulled firmly. The slimy phlegm that covered Melvin's gigantic fist was strong and gluey, but it was no match for Wedgie Power.

Captain Underpants pulled and pulled
until Miss Anthrope became completely
dislodged with a noisy, wet, disgusting
sound. (Note: Please feel free to make the
noisy, wet, disgusting sound of your choice
to emphasize the intense drama of this
gripping paragraph.)

"I'm free!" cried Miss Anthrope. "Let's
get the heck out of here!"

Suddenly, the Bionic Booger Boy reached down and grabbed Captain Underpants by the cape. The monster held on tightly with his gigantic, gooey robotic fingers.

"ACK!" cried Captain Underpants. "He's got my cape! He's got my cape!"

"Well just untie it!" screamed Miss Anthrope. "Let's GO! Let's GO!"

"But I — I can't fight crime without my cape!" cried Captain Underpants.

"*FORGET YOUR STUPID CAPE!*" Edith screamed. "Just save me, you idiot!"

CHAPTER 21
YOU CAN'T HAVE YOUR CAPE AND EDITH, TOO

As anybody will tell you, no superhero is complete without a cape. I mean, without a cape, a superhero is just a guy wearing fancy underwear (or in this case, *not*-so-fancy underwear). But Captain Underpants knew what had to be done. He reached up with his free hand and courageously untied his cape, valiantly sacrificing his aesthetic integrity to save the life of a mere mortal being.

Captain Underpants and Miss Anthrope
were now free, but they weren't safe yet. The
Bionic Booger Boy swung at our hero with
all his might. Captain Underpants weaved
around Melvin's frantic, flying, phlegm-flingin'
fists as he tried to find a safe place to land.

Suddenly, Captain Underpants's 100 percent cotton-powered vision spotted George and Harold miles away. With lightning speed, he flew down to meet the boys.

"George and Harold," said Captain Underpants, "you've got to keep this woman safe while I destroy that robotic slimeball!"

"OK," said Harold, "but hurry up — here he comes!"

"Wait," cried Miss Anthrope. "I—I didn't
get a chance to say thank you." She turned
and kissed Captain Underpants all over his
face with wet, drooly smooches.

"Thank you! Thank you! Thank you!" she
said between each sloppy kiss.

"Yuck!" said Harold.

"I sure hope she doesn't thank *us*," said George.

When Miss Anthrope had finished slobbering all over Captain Underpants's face, she gave him a great big hug for good luck. "Now go get him, tiger," she said coyly.

But Captain Underpants didn't move. He just stood there staring blankly into space.

Off in the distance, George and Harold
could hear the Bionic Booger Boy approaching.
Each thundering footstep brought the horrible
beast closer and closer, until at last he stood
towering above them, panting heavily, and
dripping profanely.

Miss Anthrope screamed and ran away.

"Hurry, Captain Underpants!" cried
Harold. "DO SOMETHING!"

"Yeah," cried George. "KICK HIS HINEY!
KICK HIS HINEY!"

But Captain Underpants didn't move.
He didn't fight. He didn't fly. He didn't kick
anybody's hiney. In fact, the only thing he
did do was get very, very angry.

"What the heck is going on here, bubs?"
he screamed. "And why am I standing here
in my underwear?"

George and Harold didn't like the sound
of that.

CHAPTER 22
WELCOME BACK, KRUPPER

If you read the comic on page 7 of this novel, then you know what happens whenever Captain Underpants gets water on his head. Unfortunately, Miss Anthrope's wet, slobbery kisses had produced the same effect.

Captain Underpants had been turned back into Mr. Krupp . . . and now he was about to be turned into *lunch*!

Quickly, George and Harold began frantically snapping their fingers.

SNAP! SNAP! SNAP! SNAP! SNAP!

Again and again, they snapped. But Mr. Krupp's face was still slimy and wet with gooey kiss juice, and the snaps were having no effect at all.

The mighty mucus monster shoved Mr.
Krupp into his gummy mouth and swallowed
him whole . . .

. . . and then he came after George and
Harold.

"HELP!" screamed George.

"WE'RE DOOMED!" screamed Harold.

CHAPTER 23
SULU SAVES THE DAY

Halfway across the city, a plucky little hamster with bionic ears heard the terrified cries of his two best pals. Quickly, Sulu jumped out of his exercise wheel and crashed through the side of his plastic cage.

Then, with a mighty leap, he bounded from the window of George and Harold's tree house.

At that very moment, Melvin was dangling George and Harold high above his mouth.

"HAW, HAW, HAW!" laughed the Bionic Booger Boy. "ME GOTS YOU AT LAST!"

"Well, good-bye, Harold," said George.

"See you later, pal," said Harold. "It was fun while it lasted."

Finally, Melvin let go of George and Harold. The two boys screamed as they fell face-first into the gooey, gaping mouth of the —

SWOOOOOOOOOOOOSH!

The next thing George and Harold knew, they were flying sideways at an incredible speed. Everything around them was a blur of motion, except for the sight of their little buddy Sulu, who had literally grabbed them from the murky mouth of death at the very last second.

"Atta boy!" cried George.

"Hooray for Sulu!" cried Harold.

Sulu set George and Harold down on the roof of a distant building, then returned to the scene of the crime. He grabbed a few oversize novelty items from the tops of some warehouses and turned to face his mortal enemy.

CHAPTER 24
THE INCREDIBLY GRAPHIC
VIOLENCE CHAPTER,
PART 2 (IN FLIP-O-RAMA™)

WARNING:

The following stunts were performed on closed streets by a highly trained professional hamster. To avoid injury, please do not grab oversize novelty items from the tops of warehouses and beat up giant monsters with them.

FLIP-O-RAMA 2

(pages 323 and 325)

Remember, flip *only* page 323.
While you are flipping, be sure you
can see the picture on page 323
and the one on page 325.
If you flip quickly, the two
pictures will start to look like
<u>one</u> *animated* picture.

Don't forget to
add your own sound-effects!

LEFT HAND HERE

CANE TOPS KEEP
FALLIN' ON MY HEAD.

RIGHT
THUMB
HERE

RIGHT
INDEX
FINGER
HERE

324

CANE TOPS KEEP
FALLIN' ON MY HEAD.

FLIP-O-RAMA 3

(pages 327 and 329)

Remember, flip *only* page 327.
While you are flipping, be sure you
can see the picture on page 327
and the one on page 329.
If you flip quickly, the two
pictures will start to look like
<u>one</u> *animated* picture.

Don't forget to
add your own sound-effects!

LEFT HAND HERE

YUMMY, YUMMY, YUMMY (I GOT GLOVE IN MY TUMMY).

**YUMMY, YUMMY,
YUMMY (I GOT GLOVE
IN MY TUMMY).**

FLIP-O-RAMA 4

(pages 331 and 333)

Remember, flip *only* page 331.
While you are flipping, be sure you
can see the picture on page 331
and the one on page 333.
If you flip quickly, the two
pictures will start to look like
<u>one</u> *animated* picture.

Don't forget to
add your own sound-effects!

LEFT HAND HERE

A HARD DAY'S BITE

RIGHT
THUMB
HERE

A HARD DAY'S BITE

CHAPTER 25
HOW TO REVERSE THE EFFECTS OF A COMBINE-O-TRON 2000 IN ONE EASY STEP

The Bionic Booger Boy was defeated. He flopped, unconscious, into a giant boogery blob that spread across several city blocks (and nearly four whole pages) as reporters surrounded his massive, oozing body.

Soon, Melvin's mother and father showed up with the Combine-O-Tron 2000. "We saw what was happening on the news," they said. "And we want the world to know that we're going to create a new machine that will reverse the process that turned our son into this monster. If we work together, it should only take a few months to build!"

"Why don't you guys just take the batteries out of that *Combine-O-Thingy* and switch 'em around?" said George. "Wouldn't that reverse the machine's effects?"

"Well," laughed Melvin's father, "obviously you don't know anything about science, little boy. You can't expect to reverse the effects of a highly complex cellular-moleculizing Combine-O-Tron just by switching the batteries around. That type of thing only happens in obnoxious children's books."

"Ahem," said George self-consciously. "Well . . . why don't you just give it a try anyway?"

"Alright," said Mr. Sneedly, rolling his eyes and smirking. He quickly switched the batteries around and powered up the machine. "But I'm only doing this to prove a point to you kids: It's not gonna work. No way. Not in a million years. And anybody who thinks it might is a complete idiot. It goes against all the popular laws of logic and science."

He aimed the newly reconfigured Combine-O-Tron 2000 at his son and fired.

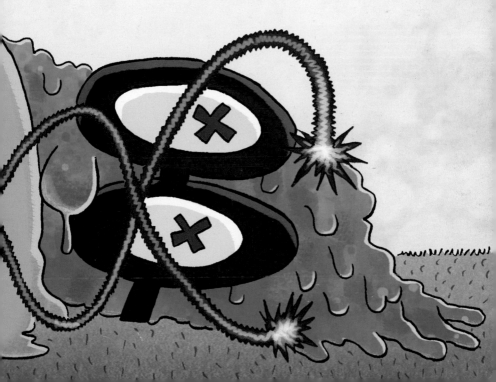

CHAPTER 26
BLAZZZZT!

Suddenly, there was a terrific explosion. The Bionic Booger Boy burst into three huge chunks of glistening snot and twisted metal, which smacked onto three nearby buildings and stuck like glue. In the center of the explosion, surrounded by smoke, stood Mr. Krupp and Melvin.

"Well, what do you know?" said Mr. Sneedly. "My idea worked."

George and Harold rolled their eyes.

"Now, step aside, kiddies," said Mrs. Sneedly as the two scientists marched off to tell the reporters all about their brilliant and inspirational scientific breakthrough.

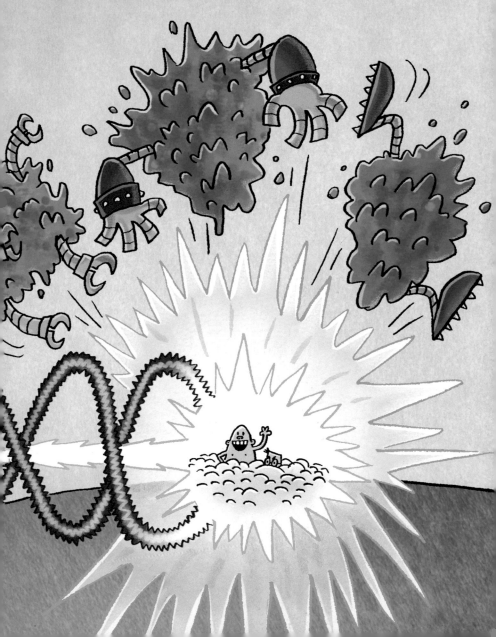

But as the smoke around Mr. Krupp and Melvin began to clear, it became obvious that they were not quite back to normal. Apparently, the newly reconfigured Combine-O-Tron 2000 had accidentally morphed Mr. Krupp and Melvin together.

"Don't worry," Mr. Sneedly told the reporters. "All I need to do is zap them one more time. That should set everything straight!" He fired up the Combine-O-Tron 2000 again and prepared to blast away.

"I sure hope this separates their bodies," said George.

"Me, too," said Harold.

BLAZZZZT!

CHAPTER 27
TO MAKE A LONG STORY SHORT

It did.

CHAPTER 28
A HAPPY ENDING

"You know something?" said George. "This is the first time one of our books actually had a happy ending."

"You're right," said Harold. "Usually they end with me screaming 'Oh, NO!' and you screaming 'Here we go again!' But we got lucky this time, I guess."

"What do you mean, *lucky*?" said Mr.
Krupp. "It was *MY* invention that saved the
world. You guys are <u>so</u> immature!"

"Huh?" said George.

"I want to see both of you bubs in my office PRONTO!" yelled Melvin. "I'm gonna punish you boys so bad, your *kids* will be born with detentions!"

"Whaaaa?" said Harold.

Suddenly, a giant extendable Octo-Claw reached out from one of the three huge chunks of boogers. It grabbed the Combine-O-Tron 2000 out of Mr. Sneedly's hands and smashed it to smithereens on the ground. Mr. and Mrs. Sneedly ran away screaming as the three humongous robotic booger chunks came to life.

Slowly, they began dripping down the sides of the buildings, each one energizing itself with a single Twin Turbo-9000 SP5 Kung-Fu Titanium/Lithium Alloy Processor.

As the huge booger chunks oozed closer
and closer, they began sprouting strange-
looking metallic eyeballs and huge,
menacing robotic limbs.

348

Suddenly, the three Ridiculous Robo-
Boogers leaped toward George, Harold,
Sulu, Mr. Krupp, and Melvin . . .

. . . and the chase was on.

"Oh, NO!" screamed Harold.

"Here we go again!" screamed George.

ABOUT THE
AUTHOR-ILLUSTRATOR

When Dav Pilkey was a kid, he was diagnosed with ADHD and dyslexia. Dav was so disruptive in class that his teachers made him sit out in the hallway every day. Luckily, Dav loved to draw and make up stories. He spent his time in the hallway creating his own original comic books — the very first adventures of Dog Man and Captain Underpants.

In college, Dav met a teacher who encouraged him to illustrate and write. He won a national competition in 1986 and the prize was the publication of his first book, WORLD WAR WON. He made many other books before being awarded the 1998 California Young Reader Medal for DOG BREATH, which was published in 1994, and in 1997 he won the Caldecott Honor for THE PAPERBOY.

THE ADVENTURES OF SUPER DIAPER BABY, published in 2002, was the first complete graphic novel spin-off from the Captain Underpants series and appeared at #6 on the USA Today bestseller list for all books, both adult and children's, and was also a New York Times bestseller. It was followed by THE ADVENTURES OF OOK AND GLUK: KUNG FU CAVEMEN FROM THE FUTURE and SUPER DIAPER BABY 2: THE INVASION OF THE POTTY SNATCHERS, both USA Today bestsellers. The unconventional style of these graphic novels is intended to encourage uninhibited creativity in kids.

His stories are semi-autobiographical and explore universal themes that celebrate friendship, tolerance, and the triumph of the good-hearted.

Dav loves to kayak in the Pacific Northwest with his wife.